Rusty

Mr. Crow

Dominic

Tom

Quinn

Meeko

Stacey

me!

My
Forever
Friends

# Friends for Keeps

# My Forever Friends

Julie Bowe

 Dial Books for Young Readers

an imprint of Penguin Group (USA) Inc.

*My special thanks to*

*Sally Walstrom, advanced-practice nurse, for answering my questions about neonatal nurseries and the babies who start their stories there. And my forever thanks to my editor, Kathy Dawson; my agent, Steven Chudney; and illustrator Jana Christy.*

DIAL BOOKS FOR YOUNG READERS
A division of Penguin Young Readers Group
Published by The Penguin Group
Penguin Group (USA) Inc., 375 Hudson Street, New York, NY 10014, U.S.A.

Penguin Group (Canada), 90 Eglinton Avenue East, Suite 700, Toronto, Ontario, Canada M4P 2Y3 (a division of Pearson Penguin Canada Inc.) • Penguin Books Ltd, 80 Strand, London WC2R 0RL, England • Penguin Ireland, 25 St. Stephen's Green, Dublin 2, Ireland (a division of Penguin Books Ltd) • Penguin Group (Australia), 250 Camberwell Road, Camberwell, Victoria 3124, Australia (a division of Pearson Australia Group Pty Ltd) • Penguin Books India Pvt Ltd, 11 Community Centre, Panchsheel Park, New Delhi - 110 017, India • Penguin Group (NZ), 67 Apollo Drive, Rosedale, Auckland 0632, New Zealand (a division of Pearson New Zealand Ltd) • Penguin Books (South Africa) (Pty) Ltd, 24 Sturdee Avenue, Rosebank, Johannesburg 2196, South Africa • Penguin Books Ltd, Registered Offices: 80 Strand, London WC2R 0RL, England

Text set in ITC Esprit
Printed in the U.S.A.
1 3 5 7 9 10 8 6 4 2

Library of Congress Cataloging-in-Publication Data
Bowe, Julie, date.
My forever friends / by Julie Bowe.
p. cm. – (Friends for keeps ; [4])
Summary: Former best friends Brooke and Jenna are feuding, and soon all the girls in the fourth-grade class are split into two groups, with Ida May right in the middle trying to put things back the way they used to be.
ISBN 978-0-8037-3513-2 (hardcover)
[1. Best friends—Fiction. 2. Friendship—Fiction. 3. Schools—Fiction.
4. Interpersonal relations—Fiction.] I. Title.
PZ7.B671943Mx 2011 [Fic]—dc22 2010038151

Books in the
**Friends for Keeps** series
by Julie Bowe

This book,
including the spiders
(especially the spiders!)
is for my son, Eli

My
Forever
Friends

# Chapter

# 1

I'm Ida May and I'm feeling a little squished. That's because I'm sitting on a piano bench between Jenna Drews and Brooke Morgan. I was saving half of the bench for my best friend, Stacey Merriweather, but Jenna budged in before Stacey could. Jenna is my sometimes friend. Then Brooke budged in on the other side of me. Brooke is my sometimes-not friend.

We're all here, at Jenna's house, for a shower. Not the wet kind. The party kind. Jenna's mom is having a baby, so Brooke's mom decided the PTA should give her a baby shower. Mrs. Drews is the PTA president. Mrs. Morgan is vice president, which means she and Mrs. Drews are supposed to get along.

"Piano benches aren't really made for *three*

people," I say, looking at Brooke. "Maybe you could sit on the floor?" There are no empty chairs left.

"I don't *do* floors," Brooke says, flicking back her long, shiny hair and nudging her butt another notch onto the bench.

I sigh and pull in my shoulders.

Jenna glances past me at Brooke. "Just *floors*?" She squints. "I didn't think you could do *anything*. Except dance around like a horse. And act like you're the boss of the world."

Brooke leans across me and squints back at Jenna. "It takes one to know one," she says. "And it's better to dance like a horse than to look like one."

"Ouch," I say, squeezing my knees.

Jenna shoots dagger eyes at Brooke.

Brooke shoots dagger eyes at Jenna.

"Hold your fire," I say, raising my hand. I slide off the bench, onto the floor, and scoot in next to Stacey.

"What's the score?" Stacey asks, glancing up at Brooke and Jenna and the empty space between them.

"Still tied," I reply. "Zero to zero."

Jenna and Brooke have been best friends

4

since kindergarten, so they've fought over lots of things before. Kickball scores. Bus seats. Lunch line positions. But this fight is different. No one knows what started it. I'm not even sure if Jenna and Brooke know, it's been going on for so long.

"Do you think they'll ever be friends again?" Stacey whispers.

I shrug. "Maybe. If one of them apologizes for whatever she did to make the other one mad."

Stacey does a snort. "Like that will ever happen."

I nod. When it comes to *not* being sorry, Jenna and Brooke are tied for first place.

Stacey gives Jenna a sparkly smile. She's an expert at doing them. Especially when she wants to change the mood or get her way. I've seen her use her sparkly smile on her mom a million times. And on our teacher, Mr. Crow. And on the boys in our class when they threaten to chase us with daddy longlegs spiders. "You're going to need a rake to clean up after *this* party!" she says brightly to Jenna. Baby clothes, toys, diapers, bottles, ribbons, and crumpled-up wrapping paper branch out around Mrs. Drews's chair.

Jenna lifts her chin. "Not my party," she snips. "Not my problem."

Even though Jenna says that, I know she doesn't mean it. She helps out a lot around here. Cleaning. Washing dishes. Taking care of her little sister, Rachel. And not just because her mom can't right now. Her parents have rules about pitching in. My parents have rules too, but sometimes they let them slip.

Nothing is slippery at Jenna's house.

"This one next, Mommy!" Rachel picks up a big box wrapped in yellow duckie paper. She rips it open and pulls back the tissue inside. Rachel is only in kindergarten, so everyone thinks it's cute that she's helping her mom with the presents. I wouldn't mind tearing open a few presents too, but when you're in fourth grade it's not so cute anymore.

Rachel pulls out a quilt that's the size of a pan of school pizza. Green and yellow with silky white trim.

"How nice," Mrs. Drews says, holding up the baby quilt for everyone to see.

All the moms coo.

Me and Stacey sigh.

"How much longer until dessert?" Stacey whispers to me.

I look at my watch. "I'd say another fifteen coos or so," I whisper back.

Brooke's foot nudges Stacey. Stacey looks up. Brooke does a fake yawn and rolls her eyes. She's an expert at making eye comments. And at dipping into other people's conversations.

Stacey does a fake yawn and rolls her eyes back. They both giggle.

"Thank you, Francine," Mrs. Drews says to an older woman sitting across the crowded room. "My sewing projects never turn out as lovely yours."

"Well," Mrs. Eddy says, her wrinkled cheeks glowing pink, "I've had sixty years of practice!"

Mrs. Drews passes the green and yellow quilt to Brooke's mom, who takes it and rubs it against her red cheek. *Fake* red. I see a smudge rub off onto the silky white trim. "It's yummy, Francine! Simply *yummy*! Honestly, I could just *eat it up*!" She laughs loudly and passes the quilt along.

All the moms do friendly chuckles.

7

Mrs. Drews zeroes in on the red smudge and makes her mouth do a smile.

Me and Stacey do nose giggles. Partly because of the *yummy* and partly because of the *Francine*. That's because *Francine* is always *Mrs. Eddy* to us. She used to be a real teacher at our school, Purdee Elementary, but now she's just a substitute. I never even knew she had a first name. But I did know that she makes nice quilts, because she's helping our class make one for the school auction in a few weeks. We're having a carnival too. If we're lucky, we'll raise enough money to buy new playground equipment. Jenna keeps reminding us that her mom is in charge of the whole thing, so of course it will be perfect.

"Pink is for girl babies and blue is for boy babies," Stacey says as she passes the little green and yellow quilt to me. "So what are green and yellow for?"

Brooke pokes in. "Those are the colors you choose when you don't know what kind of baby it will be."

*What kind of baby it will be,* I think to myself. Then I do a little snort. It's the kind of snort

Randi Peterson would do if she were about to say something clever. Randi is another girl in our class. So are Meeka and Jolene. I guess their moms aren't on the PTA, or they'd be here too.

"Green must be for frog babies," I say, and do the snort again.

Jenna crinkles her eyebrows. "Of course," she says, taking the quilt from Brooke and passing it along. "My mother is having a frog."

Stacey does the snort too. "And yellow is for . . . chicken babies!" She flaps her wings.

"Or monkey babies," I say. "Because of the bananas."

Me and Stacey do a snort duet.

Jenna flicks back her blond braids and lifts her chin. "Stop making jokes about my mother and her baby." Even though she says it to me and Stacey, she shoots a look at Brooke.

"We're not making jokes about them," I say. "We're just exercising our imaginations, like Mr. Crow is always telling us to do." Our teacher is a big fan of imagination.

Stacey scratches her armpits like a monkey. "Ooo-ooo-ooo!" she grunts.

I scratch my armpits and grunt back even though Jenna is poking me with her toe.

But I ignore her toe pokes because it feels so good to be goofing around with Stacey again.

Lately, Stacey and Brooke have been busy practicing their dance for the spring recital. They did a duet called "The Pony Dance." But now the recital is over, so Stacey isn't as busy with all the other things she likes besides me.

I hear a monkey grunt and look up. Brooke is scratching her armpits and crossing her eyes at Stacey.

Stacey giggles and crosses her eyes back. Stacey is Brooke's best friend too, so sometimes I have to share her.

I try to cross my eyes, but I'm not very good at it. Besides, Brooke and Stacey have already moved on to tongue rolling, which is even harder for me.

I'm a tiny bit glad when Mrs. Morgan sees what's going on and shoots dagger eyes at Brooke.

Brooke and Stacey uncurl their tongues and fold their hands.

No more monkey business.

When all the presents are finally unwrapped, my mom and Brooke's mom hand out cake and ice cream and punch to everyone.

Me and the other girls take our desserts outside. It's the first really warm Saturday we've had all spring. The kind that makes you feel like summer vacation is just a block or two away.

I help Rachel carry her punch. Jenna, Brooke, and Stacey speed walk past us to the picnic table that sits near the little woods behind Jenna's house. Jenna gets there first and hogs up the shade. "Ha-ha," she says, giving Brooke a smirk. "I win."

Brooke sets down her dessert and adjusts the sparkly headband that's holding her hair perfectly in place. "I'm your guest," she says to Jenna. "You're supposed to give *me* the best spot."

Jenna scoops cake and ice cream into her mouth. She chews it slowly while Brooke waits for an answer.

"I'm more of a guest than you are," Jenna finally replies. "This party is for *my* mother. You should be in the kitchen helping *your* mother cut the cake." She slips another forkful in.

Brooke does a big huff, brushes pine needles

off the bench, and plops down at the opposite end. Stacey and Rachel sit across from her. I sit between Brooke and Jenna.

"It's so unfair," Stacey says, eating her cake and ice cream. "All those presents! And the baby doesn't even know she's getting them!"

"Agreed," Brooke says. "She shouldn't get any presents until she's old enough to appreciate them. Like me." She does a sweet smile.

"They're not really for the baby," Jenna says. "They're for my mother. And we don't know if it's a girl yet, so you shouldn't call it a *she*."

"Let's hope it's a girl and not some disgusting boy," Brooke grumbles. She looks at all of us. "Have you *seen* Rusty's fingernails lately? Ugh. I swear he's still got third-grade dirt under them."

Rusty is one of the boys in our class. Quinn, Dominic, Joey, Zane, Tom, and the Dylans are the others. Most of them have dirt collections.

"Not to mention Joey Carpenter." Brooke shudders. "Talk about dis*gust*ing. He's constantly licking his fingers and touching his eyeballs." She licks frosting from her glossy lips and stabs her cake. "Now he's got Rusty doing it too. Can you imagine? I can. It's my life. I can't believe Mr. Crow stuck me in a *friendless* circle with those two apes."

A few weeks ago, Mr. Crow rearranged our desks into four clusters he calls *friendship circles.* But Brooke calls hers a *friendless* circle because she got stuck with only boys—Rusty and Joey. She even made them *friendless* bracelets on the day we were supposed to make friendship bracelets for each other. Mr. Crow gave us embroidery thread and beads to use, but Brooke dug broken rubber bands and twisty ties and fuzzy Life Savers out of her desk and made bracelets for Rusty and Joey out of that stuff instead.

She meant for Rusty and Joey to hate them, but instead they *loved* them. Or at least they pretended to. They showed the bracelets to everyone and argued over who Brooke loved more and which of them she was going to marry and how many children they would have.

When the news got back to Brooke, she ran straight to the girls' bathroom and splashed cold water on her face to keep from throwing up.

Rusty and Joey wore the friendless bracelets

until the twisty ties gave out. Then they ate the fuzzy Life Savers. But they still haven't given up on Brooke.

"My baby won't be disgusting," Rachel says, "even if it is a boy." She looks at her sister. "Right, Jen?"

Jenna huffs. "It's not up to you, Rachel. People are disgusting whether you want them to be or not."

Rachel ducks her head. "I *wish* it would be a boy," she mumbles, stirring her ice cream and cake into a muddy puddle. "I got enough sisters."

Jenna gives Rachel a squint. Then she looks up suddenly and tilts her head toward the house. "Hmm," she says, pretending to listen. "I think I hear Mom calling for you, Rachel."

"Really?" Rachel says, listening too.

Jenna cups her hand to her ear. "Something about . . . more cake."

Rachel's face brightens. "Maybe the baby doesn't want his!" She scrambles up from her bench and scampers toward the house. Then she stops and looks back at us. "You guys stay put 'til I get back!" she shouts.

Jenna puffs her lips as we watch Rachel disappear into the house. "She's such a boss," she says. "But at least she fell for it. Come on. Time to go."

"Go where?" Stacey asks.

"To the park," Jenna replies.

"Ew," Brooke says. "Grass. Trees. Bugs. Dis-*gust*ing."

"What about Rachel?" I ask.

"Fourth graders only," Jenna says. "And their dogs."

Jenna disappears into her garage while I pile up the paper plates and cups and toss them into a garbage can by the back door. A moment later Jenna returns with her little dog, Biscuit, yipping and pulling on the end of his leash.

I follow everyone down a path that goes through the woods behind Jenna's house. I've walked it with Jenna a bunch of times because it's a shortcut between our neighborhood and the Purdee Town Park.

"Stay on the path," Jenna reminds us. "Or this place will eat you alive."

Jenna is a big fan of walking around in nature, as long as nature doesn't walk around, on, or near her. Ticks. Spiders. Poison ivy. Hungry bears. She's always reminding us to stay on the path or suffer the consequences.

Secretly, I think if I had a little woods behind my house I would wander around in it all the time. I would pack my sketchbook and Choco Chunks and my sock monkey, George. George could climb a tree and keep a lookout for bears while I sit underneath and draw pictures. I would just be sure to wear bug spray and long pants. And try not to smell like honey.

Jenna's leading the way, but halfway through the woods, Biscuit stops and sniffs at a crooked path that veers off from the main path to the park.

"Where does that trail go?" Stacey asks.

Brooke is about to answer when Jenna yanks Biscuit's leash, nearly pushing Brooke over. Accidentally on purpose.

"It goes *nowhere*," Jenna snaps. "Right, Brooke?"

Brooke catches her balance, huffs, and punches her fists into her hips. "Didn't your mother ever teach you any manners?"

Jenna turns back to Brooke. "My mother is too busy being president of the PTA and chairperson of the school auction *and* carnival to teach me anything. This will be the best fund-raiser our school has ever had because she's in charge of it."

"Give it up, Jenna," Brooke grumbles, pushing past me and pulling Stacey along. "Your mom isn't a superhero. She can't do everything and still sit around the house, waiting for the baby to be born."

Brooke and Stacey prance down the main path toward the park.

Jenna tugs Biscuit, following after them.

I wait until Brooke's sparkly headband and Stacey's dark curls and Jenna's bobbing braids disappear behind the trees.

Then I turn and squint down the crooked path.

"It must go somewhere," I say to myself, "or there wouldn't be a path."

I take a step and squint harder, but I can't see very far because of all the trees.

"C'mon, Ida!" I hear Jenna shout from far away.

I turn back toward the main path, but I stop again when a breeze catches my bangs and a tiny sound catches my ears.

*Clink . . . clink . . . rattle . . . clink . . .*

Something clinky is down that path.

Something rattly.

Like finger bones. Ones that are still wearing rings.

A moment later the breeze is gone and so is the sound.

But it stays inside my head. Right next to the idea that Jenna has a secret at the end of that crooked path.

A secret that Brooke knows about.

"Ida!" Jenna calls again.

I hurry to catch up.


Everyone is ready to leave when we get back to Jenna's house. I help my mom load up the punch bowl and cake containers, and wave good-bye to Jenna and Rachel.

"There's something I need to ask you," Mom says as we drive home.

I flick my sparkly earlobes. "I'm all ears," I reply, and do a clever smile.

Mom glances at me. "Mrs. Drews needs extra rest until the baby's born, so she's wondering if

Jenna and Rachel can come to our house more often."

I stop flicking. "How often?"

"After school for starters. Weekends if Mr. Drews can find some extra work." Mom glances at me again. "Is that okay with you?"

If Mom had asked me that question a year ago I would have said *"No way."* Jenna used to be super-mean to me until I finally stood up to her. Then things got better. Not perfect, but better.

"Will it help the baby?" I ask.

Mom nods. "It's a complicated pregnancy, so it's important that Mrs. Drews can rest as much as possible. She even asked Brooke's mom to take over as chairperson of the school auction and carnival."

My chin drops. *"Brooke's* mom is in charge now?"

"Mmm-hmm," Mom says. "Why? Is that bad?"

I close my mouth and lean back, thinking about how Jenna will feel when she finds out her mom isn't in charge anymore.

And how Brooke will feel when she finds out her mom *is*.

"It's only bad if you're Jenna Drews," I mumble.

Mom pulls into our driveway and turns off the car. "So is it okay with you? Jenna and Rachel coming over after school?"

I shrug. "I guess."

"Good," Mom says. "Because we start on Monday."

# Chapter

# 2

"I should warn you," I say to George on Monday morning. "Jenna and Rachel are coming over after school."

The last time they were here, Rachel put an old doll dress on George. Tied ribbons to his tail. Snapped barrettes on his ears. He tried to be a good sport about it, but even a sock monkey has his limits.

"I could hide you . . ." I say, picking him up.

George brightens.

"But that's no good. They'll be coming over every day for weeks and weeks. You can't live under my bed forever, George. Besides, you have to face your fears, remember? That's what you're always telling me."

I set George on my bed and straighten his tail. "See you after school?" I say.

George gives me the silent treatment.

I look around my room. Then I gather up all my barrettes and shove them into my underwear drawer.

I turn back to George. "I took care of the barrettes," I say. "But I can't make any promises about ribbons and doll dresses."

George just glances away.

I sigh and head out the door.

Sometimes nothing you do for a friend feels like enough.


"We have a lot going on between now and the end of the school year, so I made a list," Mr. Crow says as Jolene and I finish feeding Spud, our class hamster, later at school. Jolene is my favorite partner for this because she knows furry creatures with beady eyes scare me a little. She catches Spud. I change his food and water. Before she puts him in his cage again, she always remembers to hold him extra tight so I can pet his back.

I sit down at my friendship circle. Stacey, Jenna, and Dominic are in my circle too.

Jenna straightens up and smiles as Mr. Crow points to the chalkboard. She loves lists.

- Make quilt to sell at school auction
- Class trip to Laura Ingalls Wilder Museum
- Help with games at school carnival

"Each friendship circle will help with one of the carnival game booths," Mr. Crow explains after reading the last item on the list.

"Ooo . . . dibs on dart throw!" Zane shouts.

"Rifle range!" Quinn adds.

"Dunk the principal!" Randi tosses in. She stands up and does high fives with Quinn and some of the other boys. She's practically one of them.

Mr. Crow holds up his hand. "The PTA will be choosing the games and organizing the booths. So no darts. No rifles. No dunks."

Everyone slumps.

"Great," Randi mumbles, plopping into her chair again. "Duck pond. Clothespin drop. Lollypop pull."

"Will the prizes be any good?" Rusty asks.

"Of course they will," Jenna pipes in. "My mother already bought them. She's in charge of the entire auction and carni—"

I give Jenna's knee a nudge. But it's too late.

"Um . . . *hello*?" Brooke waves her hand at Jenna. "*Your* mom isn't in charge anymore. *My* mom is." She counts off on her fingers. "The auction. The carnival games. The *prizes,* thank goodness. All your mom got so far are pencils and butterscotch candies. *Ugh.* With *my* mom in charge we'll have fake tattoos, lip gloss rings, jawbreakers . . . the list goes on and on."

Jenna sits back and steams.

"Yeah, listen to Brookey," Joey says, making puppy-dog eyes at her. "She's always right."

"Ugh-ugh!" Rusty nods and pounds a freckled fist against his chest. "Me love tattoo! Me love jawbreaker! Me love Brookey!"

Everyone giggles.

Brooke sits back and steams too.

"As I was saying," Mr. Crow continues, "we have a lot to do. Quilt, starting today. Class trip next week."

Everyone slumps again.

The fourth-grade class trip is the same every

year. Tour the Laura Ingalls Wilder Museum in Pepin, Wisconsin, and see the Little House in the Big Woods where she was born.

Supposedly, it's not the real log cabin where she lived with Ma, Pa, Mary, and baby Carrie. That one wore out a long time ago. The cabin we'll see is called a *replica*. It sounds like a cool dinosaur name, but really it's just another word for *fake*.

No one is exactly excited about seeing Laura's fake log cabin. Or touring a museum. We heard from Brooke's older sister, Jade, that it's almost as boring as a tour of the Purdee State Bank. That's where we went in second grade.

The bank tour *was* boring, even though they gave us souvenir coin purses. The plastic kind that smell like Barbies when you pinch them open. Before she moved away, Elizabeth, my last best friend, and I used to pretend that ours were toothless pet sharks. We'd take them swimming and let them gum our noses to death.

But there are no souvenir coin purses at the Laura Ingalls Wilder Museum. Jade said there are only old pots and pans and faded quilts and worn-out boots that you are not allowed to touch.

Mr. Crow glances at the clock above his desk. "That's enough chatter for now," he says. "Let's get our work done this morning so Mrs. Eddy can start teaching us how to make a quilt this afternoon."

"We already made one," Randi says, looking around at all of us. "Remember? In first grade."

Tom nods. "A construction-paper quilt," he says. "We colored it with crayons and stapled it to the bulletin board."

Jenna huffs. "Construction-paper quilts are for babies."

"I wouldn't recommend it," Tom says, blinking at Jenna. "They'll chew it up."

Jenna groans. "Duh, Tom. I meant that we would *be* babies if we made one in fourth grade."

"Technically, we're almost in *fifth* grade," Tom replies.

Jenna groans again and gives up.

Tom grins. He used to be afraid of Jenna, like me, but lately he's figured out that he has a secret weapon. I call it *The Twister*. That's because Tom can take anything Jenna says and twist it around until it means something else. Which gets Jenna all twisted up too. Still, she has a secret crush on him. I'm the only one who knows. And she's the only one who knows about my secret crush on Quinn. That's something we're both good at. Keeping secrets.

"Mrs. Eddy is an expert quilter," Mr. Crow says. "She'll help us make a real quilt out of cloth, not paper."

Meeka sits up. "With needles?"

"And scissors and thread," Mr. Crow says, nodding.

Meeka smiles. She loves things that poke and cut because she wants to be a doctor someday.

"My mom helped me sew a quilt for my dolls once," Jolene puts in.

Quinn grunts. "Girly."

"Yeah," Dominic adds. "My *grandmother* sews quilts."

"This project is for everyone—girls *and* boys," Mr. Crow says, crossing his arms. "And it will mean cooperating, not complaining. The nicer our quilt, the higher the bid. And the more money we raise at the school auction, the sooner we'll get our new playground equipment."

Everyone nods. We can't wait to have new loopy slides and a climbing wall and even a swinging bridge that will be perfect for running across with your best friend.

Dominic lifts a shoulder. "I'm in," he mumbles. "But it still sounds girly."


"Move up!" Quinn shouts from the playground pitcher's mound later, at phys ed. He waves to his teammates in the outfield.

Jolene hurries toward the baseline. So does one of the Dylans. Rusty ditches third base and stands in line with Quinn. "C'mon, Ida!" he calls, holding out his hands. "Right to me!"

I give Rusty a squint as I walk toward home plate. I hate this part of kickball. Not the kicking part. I like hearing the *thunk!* Feeling my foot sting. Running as fast as I can.

But I hate how everyone assumes I won't kick it very far. Not that I ever have. But that doesn't mean I never will.

"Do it, Ida!" Randi shouts as she rocks back and forth in her sneakers, guarding first base. She's captain of the other team. "Show us what you got!"

I give Randi a grin. She's the kind of player who wants her team to work for a win.

"Yeah, you show 'em, Ida!" Stacey calls from the grassy sidelines where our team is sitting. She gives me a quick smile, then goes back to making dandelion chains with Brooke.

I feel a tug on my arm. "Just don't pop it," Jenna says, coming up behind me. "And *don't* kick it to third, or Zane will never score."

I glance at third base. Zane leans toward us, a dandelion tucked behind his ear and his sneakers revving up for a quick dash home.

"Will this be our last out?" Brooke asks loudly as I step up to the plate and Jenna heads back to the sidelines. "I hope so. Ginormous ants are crawling all over me! Someone should get me a chair. I *am* the team captain."

"A chair?" Jenna replies as she sits on the grass a few feet away from Brooke and Stacey. "I thought witches preferred sitting on brooms."

"You can sit on my lap, Brookey," Joey says, stretching out his bony legs and patting his scabby knees. He bats his eyes at Brooke.

"I'd rather sit on *Ant Mountain*," Brooke snips.

She throws a dandelion at Joey. Stacey pitches in.

Rusty snort-laughs from the infield.

"Ready, Ida?" Quinn smiles at me from the pitcher's mound.

"As I'll ever be," I say.

Quinn tosses the ball. Slower than he did for Zane. Less bouncy.

I run a few steps and kick.

*Thunk!*

The ball pops right over Rusty's head and bounces toward third. Just what Jenna told me not to do.

"Run, Ida, run!" Jenna shouts.

So I do.

So does Zane.

So does Rusty, chasing after the ball.

"Safe!" Ms. Stein, our phys ed teacher, shouts a moment later as Zane beats Rusty to home plate. "Game's tied. Three to three."

Randi pats my back when I get to first. "Told ya you could do it."

I glance at Jenna. She gives me a nod.

"You-hoo! Ida!" Meeka calls from second base. She crouches down and dusts off the white square she's guarding. Then she picks a dandelion and holds it out to me. Meeka likes to make you feel welcome when you stop by her base.

"I'll be there in a minute," I call back.

And I am.

Then Joey kicks me to third.

And Jenna kicks me home.

"Safe!" Ms. Stein shouts as I cross the plate. "We're out of time. Team Morgan wins. Four to three."

Brooke and Stacey do a victory dance. Meeka and Jolene join in, even though they didn't win.

My back tingles from all the friendly slaps. My ears ring from all the squeals. My neck itches from the dandelion necklace Stacey put on me. I can't stop smiling. Not even while I'm eating Mrs. Kettleson's goulash at lunch with the other girls. I've eaten it lots of times before, but never with a smile.

"That was the first kickball score of my whole fourth-grade life," I say to Jenna as we carry our trays up to the dish room window.

"I know," Jenna replies. "Do it ten more times and you'll be as good as me."

When we get back to our classroom, Mrs. Eddy is waiting for us. Quilts are draped over the desks in each of our friendship circles. My group's has a pretty pattern of squares and triangles.

Mrs. Eddy walks around the room and tells us about each of the quilts. One looks like a big colorful star. Another one has flowers everywhere. It's called a *rose quilt*. One is a jumble of different shapes and patterns and colors. There's stuff sewn on it too. Lace. Buttons. A tiny silver spoon.

"This was from my wedding dress," Mrs. Eddy explains, running her crooked fingers over the lace that's sewn on the jumbled-up quilt. "The buttons came from my husband's old army uniform. And the spoon belonged to our son when he was a baby."

"What's that in the corner?" Stacey asks, pointing to the quilt. "It looks like—"

"A spider!" Jolene cries excitedly. She loves animals. Even the creepy kind.

"That's right," Mrs. Eddy says, pointing to a little spider made out of black thread that's sewn to a silvery web.

"Ta-*ranch*-u-la!" Joey says, wiggling his fingers.

Everyone laughs.

"Yuck," Brooke says. "Who would want a spider on their quilt?"

Mrs. Eddy smiles at Brooke. "Spiders are a sign of good luck," she says.

Brooke huffs. "*Bad* luck, if you ask me."

She glances at Jenna.

Jenna glances back.

It makes me wonder if they know something about spiders that the rest of us don't.

"This type of quilt is called a *crazy quilt*," Mrs. Eddy continues. "Can anyone guess why?"

Joey raises his hand. "Because *girls* made it?"

All the boys snort.

"Yeah, all quilts are crazy because they're *all* made by girls!" Quinn puts in.

All the girls grumble.

"Actually," Mrs. Eddy says, "in some ancient cultures it was the *men* who made the quilts." She gives Quinn a look over the top of her glasses.

"Huh?" Quinn says.

Mrs. Eddy opens a big book she brought along. "And medieval soldiers wore armor made from quilted fabric." She holds up a picture of a knight riding into battle.

"Cool," Dominic says, sitting up higher in his chair.

"Quilts were used to wrap dead bodies for burial when coffins weren't available," Mrs. Eddy continues, flipping to a picture of pioneers in covered wagons.

"Ew," Brooke says.

"Awesome," Randi adds.

"And then, of course, there's the Kentucky Graveyard Quilt," Mrs. Eddy says, closing the book and hugging it to her chest. "But you wouldn't be interested in that." She glances at Quinn.

"The Whoyard What?" Quinn asks, scrambling to his knees.

A smile flits between Mr. Crow and Mrs. Eddy. She flips open her book again.

"The Kentucky Graveyard Quilt was made by a woman named Elizabeth Roseberry Mitchell in 1843 to keep track of the deaths in her family." Mrs. Eddy shows us a picture of the quilt. "She sewed little coffins along the edge," Mrs. Eddy explains, pointing to the picture. "One for each member of her family. When someone died, she moved his or her coffin to the graveyard." Mrs. Eddy taps on a fenced-in square at the center of the quilt.

Quinn's jaw drops.

"Creepy," Randi says. "I *like* it."

Mrs. Eddy walks around the room, giving everyone a closer look at all those coffins. "Are quilts still too *girly* for you, young man?" she asks when she gets to Quinn's desk.

Quinn gulps and shakes his head. "No, ma'am," he says. "I'm *dying* to make one."

Mrs. Eddy chuckles. "Good," she says. "Because I'll be back next week to get you started."

"Awh," one of the Dylans says. "Can't we start today?"

"Yeah, let's do the graveyard one!" Joey puts in.

"No," Mrs. Eddy replies, closing her book. "I have another design in mind. It's called a friendship tree."

Jenna suddenly straightens up. "Did you say . . . *tree?*"

Mrs. Eddy nods. "And friendship. You'll see what I mean next week."

# Chapter

# 3

"I've got the whole week scheduled out," Jenna says, pulling a clipboard from her backpack when we get to my front porch after school. A chart is clipped to the front.

Five rows: Monday, Tuesday, Wednesday, Thursday, Friday.

Three columns: Snack, Game, Craft.

Rachel pokes in for a look. Then she runs inside.

"See?" Jenna says, pointing to the first row on her chart. "Today is Monday, so that means our *snack* is peanut butter toast. Our *game* is a scavenger hunt. And our *craft* is wind chimes. I already made maps for the game. The boundaries are marked in red."

Jenna sits on the steps and shuffles three

maps to the top of her clipboard. "If you go out of bounds, you automatically lose."

"Nice," I say, sitting next to her and pinching up one of the maps. "Very organized."

"I know," Jenna says. "It's one of my talents."

"Not mine," I say, reading all the notes Jenna has written on the map. "Does it really take fourteen giant steps to get from my porch to the edge of my front yard?"

"Mmm-hmm," Jenna replies, straightening the papers on her clipboard.

"Huh," I say, studying the map again. "And I had no idea poisonous snakes potentially live under the bushes by my sandbox." I glance at Jenna. "Thanks for letting me know."

Jenna nods. "That's why I'm here," she says. "To keep you safe."

She takes the map back and clips it under her activity chart.

I do a little smile. There are things about Jenna I'd like to change. Her bossiness. The way she treats Rachel sometimes. Her grudge against Brooke. But there's one thing I wouldn't change. Jenna knows her talents and she isn't afraid to tell you.

"Wind chimes are cool," I say, looking at the chart. "My grandma has some that are made out of seashells."

"Ours won't be," Jenna says, pulling a tangled lump of sticks and string from the bottom of her backpack. Shiny nuts, bolts, and screws dangle from the string as she untangles everything. "We're making our wind chimes just like this one. I made it last summer at camp."

The more Jenna untangles, the more I hear a sound I recognize.

*Clink . . . clink . . . rattle . . . clink . . .*

The same sound I heard coming from the crooked path in her little woods.

I study Jenna for a moment. "Grandma May hangs her wind chimes on her porch," I say. "Where do you hang *yours*?"

"Um . . . by my . . . door," Jenna says.

"Really?" I say. "I've never noticed them before. Back door or front door?"

"Neither," Jenna mumbles, running her tongue across her lips. She quickly sets the wind chimes by her backpack, grabs her clipboard, and stands up. "Come on, or we'll get behind schedule." She heads inside before I can ask any more questions.

Mom listens patiently while Jenna explains the activity chart to her. Then she points to the toaster and gets out of the kitchen.

"Ida, get the bread," Jenna says. "I'll run the toaster. Rachel can spread the peanut butter."

"I want jelly too," Rachel says, setting George on the counter. She folds a paper towel into a triangle and tapes it on him like a diaper.

"No, Rachel," Jenna replies. "The snack for today is peanut butter toast, *not* jelly toast." She taps her schedule with a butter knife.

Rachel cradles George and crinkles her nose. "Creamy or chunky?"

I toss a loaf of bread onto the counter and pull a jar of peanut butter out of a cupboard. "Chunky," I say, reading the label.

Rachel stomps her foot.

"We've got jelly too." I set the peanut butter next to the bread. "Should I get it?"

Rachel nods and bounces George to her shoulder. She pats him on the back and peeks inside his diaper.

Jenna huffs. She unclips a pen from her chart

and writes *And jelly* next to *Peanut butter toast.* "But this is the only change you're allowed," she says, frowning at Rachel.

"Thank you," Rachel replies. Then she does a fake burp. "Good boy, George!" She hugs my monkey tight. "I love George!" she cries. "Even more than jelly."

"He's the best monkey around," I say. "The only one, actually. I've had him forever."

"Then him and you are forever friends," Rachel replies.

I nod. "Just like you and Jenna."

Rachel laughs. "We're not friends. We're sisters."

Jenna puts two slices of bread into the toaster. "Rachel's right," she says. "Being sisters is different than being friends. Harder. Especially when you're the *big* sister."

"Being friends is hard too," I say. "Especially when they don't stick together." I'm thinking about Jenna and Brooke, but I'm also thinking about me and Stacey. Lately, we haven't been as sticky as we used to be.

"That's what I mean," Jenna says. "When you're sisters, you have to stick together no matter what.

When you're friends, you can ditch each other. Especially when the other one stabs you in the back."

She doesn't mention Brooke's name, but I bet that's the stabber she's thinking of.

"Nu-uh, Jenna," Rachel says, shaking her head. "When you're *forever* friends you can't ditch each other. It's almost as bad as being sisters."

The toast pops. Rachel spreads peanut butter on one slice and jelly on the other. We split it three ways.

It doesn't take very long to find everything on Jenna's scavenger hunt list. Sticks. Rocks. Worms. Dead bugs. We meet on my porch after the hunt and set the stuff we found by the boxes of baby flowers my dad bought yesterday. He's going to plant them in the big clay pots that sit on our porch steps every spring. Me and my mom painted the pots when I was little. Bright flowers. Rainbows. Butterflies.

Jenna checks off Monday's snack and game on her chart and then hands out the sticks we collected and the screws and string and other stuff she brought along for making wind chimes.

"Tomorrow we play hide-and-seek," Jenna says,

tying a long silver screw to a knobby stick. "Rain or shine. And our craft will be seed collages."

"Yay!" Rachel says as she slips donut-shaped nuts onto her string like beads on a necklace. "Seed colleges are my best craft!"

"*Collages,*" Jenna says, correcting her. "But you have piano lessons tomorrow, so you can't make one. If we don't start right away the glue won't have time to dry."

Rachel slumps. Nuts spill off her string and pitter-patter down the steps. "No fair," she grumbles.

"We could wait until my mom's done giving Rachel her lesson and let the collages dry overnight," I offer.

Rachel straightens up. "Yeah, we could do that! Because I *really* want to make a seed college. For my baby's room!"

"The baby already has enough stuff in that room, Rachel," Jenna says.

"Yeah, but Mommy says the smaller you are, the more stuff you need."

"Listen, if you *stuff* one more thing in that kid's room, the door won't shut."

"But Mommy says—"

"*Mommy says . . . Mommy says . . .*" Jenna mocks. "Stop bugging Mom about every little thing. No wonder she's sick."

Rachel blinks at Jenna for a moment. Her throat clicks. "Mommy's sick?"

"Duh, Rachel," Jenna replies, tying another bolt to her string. "Why do you think she has to ship us off to Ida's house every day? Because the baby is making her *sick*. And your pestering doesn't help one bit. It only reminds her how much she wishes things would go back to the way they used to be. Before the stupid baby came along."

Rachel's eyes go bright with tears. She grabs George and jumps up. "My baby's *not* stupid!" she shouts at Jenna. "*You* are!" Then she stomps across the porch and into the house. Nuts and bolts roll away.

Jenna doesn't say anything.

I set down my wind chimes and stand up. "We'd better go talk to her."

"I've got nothing to say," Jenna replies, scooping up Rachel's scattered nuts and bolts.

I frown. "How about 'I'm sorry'?" I suggest.

Jenna looks up. "Sorry for what?" she asks. "I told her the truth. You want me to apologize for that?"

"No, not for *telling* her the truth. For the *way* you told her. Your voice was mean."

Jenna laughs. "I didn't choose my voice, Ida. It came with the rest of me. Package deal. I can't help it if I'm not all sparkly and sugar-coated like Stacey."

I sigh and go looking for Rachel.

I find her in the backyard, talking to George and digging holes with a faded plastic shovel in the sandbox my dad built for me when I was little. It's been so long since I've played in it, weeds are growing around the edges.

"You're lucky, George," I hear Rachel say as I walk toward her. "You don't got a sister. Just Ida."

"What are you doing?" I ask, crouching next to her.

Rachel looks up. Her eyes are red. A streak of snot shines on her cheek. "Making a garden," she grumbles. "*Not* a seed college. Tomorrow, I'm planting *my* seeds here."

I watch Rachel turn over the sand again and

again with the shovel. Then she pats it smooth.

"Sometimes I help my dad plant stuff," I say, glancing at a purple patch of flowers in a shady corner by my house. "But never in the sandbox. I think mostly just weeds grow here."

"I don't care," Rachel says. "I'll plant my seeds even if they grow up to be weeds."

Rachel stands and brushes sand off her fingers. "Do you got any water?" she asks.

I nod.

Rachel helps me get a watering can from the shed and we fill it with a hose.

Then we lug the water to the sandbox and start pouring it out like rain.

A minute later, flip-flops snap up behind us.

"What's *she* doing?"

I glance back at Jenna. "Making a garden," I say.

"A *garden*?" Jenna huffs. She crosses her arms and watches Rachel drown the sandbox. "Flowers don't grow in sand, you know."

Rachel keeps watering and humming.

"She knows," I say. "But she's planting them anyway."

Jenna huffs again and taps her flip-flop against the edge of the sandbox. "Stop it, Rachel," she says. "You're being stupid."

I give Jenna a frown.

She sighs. "I mean, your *idea* is stupid. Nothing grows in sand."

Rachel looks up, but she doesn't say anything. She takes the empty watering can back to the hose and starts filling it up again.

"So what if nothing grows?" I say to Jenna. "It doesn't hurt to try."

Jenna gives me a squint. "Yes it does. It hurts a lot when things don't go your way. I should know."

"Lots of things go your way, Jenna," I say.

"Like what?"

I think for a moment. "You only got one wrong on our spelling quiz today. That was second-best in the whole class."

"Tom didn't get *any* wrong. That was first-best."

"Stacey gave you her brownie at lunch."

"She didn't give it to me. She offered it to everyone. I only got it because nobody else likes walnuts."

I think some more. "Brooke chose you first for kickball."

"Duh, Ida," Jenna says. "She wanted her team to win. If Randi hadn't been captain of the other team, she would have chosen her first, not me."

"Still, you're the second-best kickball player in our class."

"Who wants to be second-best?" Jenna says. "I'm not first-best at anything."

"You're Brooke's first-best friend," I say. "At least, you used to be. And you could be again if you'd tell her you're sorry."

"For what?"

"For whatever you two are fighting about. What *are* you fighting about? Do you even know?"

"Of course I know," Jenna replies. "I'm not stupid. And I'm *not* apologizing. She should."

"Maybe she would, if you went first. Then you'd be the first-best apologizer."

I do a clever smile.

Jenna does a squint.

Her flip-flops snap away.

# Chapter

## 4

"Did my mom call your mom yet?" Stacey asks on Friday morning when we sit down at our friendship circle. "*Pleeease* say yes!" She clutches her hands to her chest.

"*Pleeease* don't spit," Dominic says, wiping his glasses.

I smile at Stacey. "Yes," I say. "She did."

Stacey squeals. "So can I spend the weekend with you?" she asks, butt hopping. "*Pleeease* say yes again!"

Dominic scoots away.

"Yes again!" I reply.

Stacey butt hops like crazy. "Lucky us!" she cries.

"Lucky me," Dominic grumbles.

"Yep," I say. "We're luckier than . . . *spiders!*"

"Spiders?" Jenna walks up to our friendship circle. She slips off a sandal and swings it over Dominic's head. "Where? I'll get them!"

Dominic ducks. "Hey!"

"No spiders!" I tell Jenna, waving my hands like windshield wipers. "I was just saying we're lucky because Stacey gets to spend the *whole* weekend at my house!"

"Oh," Jenna says, dropping her sandal.

Dominic sighs.

Jenna sits down. She looks at Stacey. "How come?" she asks.

Stacey stops bouncing. She picks up her gel pen and doodles a flower on her math book cover. "My mom has to work."

Jenna's jaw shifts. "So why don't you go to your dad's house?" she asks. "Or Brooke's?"

"Pick me, pick me!" Brooke bubbles from her friendless circle. It's right next to ours.

Stacey smiles at Brooke. Then she shrugs at Jenna. "I can't go to my dad's. Something came up. And I went to Brooke's house last time, so it's Ida's turn."

"No fair, no fair." Brooke pouts.

Stacey's dad lives in another town because he and her mom got divorced. Stacey's supposed to stay with her dad on the weekends, but sometimes he's too busy to take care of her, so she gets to stay here instead.

"Yippee for me," I say, and do a butt hop.

Stacey smiles and does one back.

Brooke joins in.

"Here we go again," Dominic says. "Butt hop city."

"Sit still and listen up," Jenna says to us, slipping her sandal back on. "Merry-go-round good-byes at recess. Ida, tell Randi. Stacey, tell Meeka. I'll remind Jolene."

All week, Jenna has been marching us around the playground to say our last good-byes to the old equipment that's going to get taken down to make room for the new stuff. Monday, we officially said good-bye to the swings. Tuesday, the slides. Wednesday, we did ceremonial grunts and armpit scratches on the monkey bars. And yesterday, we chanted our last round of *Buster, Buster, Buster Brown, what will you give me if I let you down?* on the teeter-totters. Today, it's the merry-go-round. Monday, the bouncy horse and seal.

"Like we don't already know, Jenna," Brooke sasses. "You handed out flyers yesterday."

Stacey nods. "And the day before that."

Dominic snorts. "And the day before *that*."

Jenna squints. "Girls only, *Dumb*inic." She pulls more flyers out of her desk and hands them around. "Tell the others to meet at the pigpen, like always. I'll begin the procession from there."

The pigpen is what everyone calls a circle of hedges on our playground. Mr. Benson, the school custodian, trimmed them to look like hogs. Hedgehogs . . . pigpen. Get it?

Brooke looks over her flyer. She wrinkles her nose. "These would look a lot better if you added some sparkly stickers, Jenna. And you should have outlined the words with a fluorescent marker. That's what I would have done."

"Me too," Stacey chimes in.

"You're not in charge of *this* ceremony, Brooke, I am," Jenna says. "No sparkles or fluorescent anything. Nothing *broken*. No one *shoved*."

Brooke stiffens. "If anyone is in charge of shoving, it's *you*, Jenna."

"Ooo . . ." Dominic says, perking up. "Fight . . . fight . . . fight . . ."

"What time, exactly, do we meet at the pig-pen?" I ask quickly. I already know the answer, but it seems like a good time to change the subject.

"Same as always," Jenna says, glancing from Brooke to me. "Morning recess. Read your flyer."

"Do we *have* to wear the crepe-paper crowns again?" Stacey asks. "Please say *no.*"

"Yes," Jenna replies.

Stacey slumps.

Brooke groans. "It would be one thing if they were real tiaras, Jenna. But crepe-paper crowns? We're only going to wear them for so long before we all start saying . . . *'So long.'* Understand?"

"Perfectly," Jenna replies, counting out three more flyers for Randi, Meeka, and Jolene. "Send me a postcard."

Brooke rolls up her flyer like a baton and taps it against her chin. "You talk big, Jenna Drews, but if I wasn't here, you'd be nobody." She points the baton around the room. "Randi . . . Meeka . . . Jolene . . . all the girls. They like *me* best. If I go, they go."

I look around. Randi is joking with Rusty. Meeka and Jolene are playing with the hamster. Stacey has gone back to doodling on her math book.

*Do* they like Brooke best?

Maybe.

Do *I*?

No.

In fact, lately, I like her worst.

"So are you coming to the pigpen at recess, or are you turning in your crown now?" Jenna asks her.

Brooke taps her chin again and thinks for a moment. "I'll play along for today. But only because I get to say good riddance to that stupid *scary*-go-round. Who would ever invent a ride that ties your hair and stomach in knots? Some boy, probably."

"Brooke's right," Tom says, walking past us just as the bell rings. "The earliest version of a merry-go-round was used by soldiers to train for battle."

"See?" Brooke says, shaking her baton at Jenna. "I'm no tinsel brain. I'm as smart as Tom. *Smarter* even, because *he* was dumb enough to *be* a boy."

Brooke laughs at her own funniness.

Tom frowns.

"Now who's talking big?" Jenna says to Brooke. "Tom's smarter than you. Everyone knows that."

"Thank you, Jenna," Tom says. "That's the nicest thing you've ever said to me."

Jenna fidgets. Her face goes red. "I wasn't talking to you, Tom," she mumbles. "I was talking to Miss Smartypants over there."

"Still," I say to Jenna, "you think Tom is the smartest kid in our class, don't you?"

I know it's a tiny bit mean to put Jenna on the spot, especially when Tom is her secret crush. But maybe if I get her thinking about something else, she'll stop fighting with Brooke.

Tom blinks and waits for Jenna's answer.

Jenna turns even redder. "If you don't count *me,* then . . . yes. He's the smartest."

Brooke snorts. "Hide your scissors, people. We wouldn't want to accidentally pop Jenna's *ginormous* head."

Tom gives Jenna a smile and walks to his desk.

I finish folding my flyer into an airplane and sail it to Randi's desk just as Mr. Crow gets ready to teach us something new.

Randi unfolds the airplane, reads it, and gives me a thumbs-up.

I give her one back.

Randi is the best at playing along, even if it involves wearing crepe paper.

"The merry-go-round good-byes were great," I say to Jenna as we sit down at my kitchen table after school. "I loved how our crepe-paper streamers waved like mermaid hair when we really got spinning. Too bad Randi's crown went flying. Tree branches and crepe paper don't mix."

Jenna nods, spreading old newspaper out in front of her. "I'll make her a new one over the weekend. She'll need it for our final ceremony on Monday. It'll be my best one ever. You'll see."

Jenna pulls our afternoon activity chart out of her backpack and looks it over. "So far we've made wind chimes, seed collages, sun catchers, and dandelion necklaces. Today we make noodle frames."

The back door slams open. Rachel walks in wiping her wet hands on her jeans. She's been watering the sandbox since she planted her collage seeds there on Tuesday.

Jenna glances up. "Oh goodie," she mumbles. "Miss Beanstalk is back."

"No flowers yet," Rachel announces, shutting the door and sliding in next to me.

I give Rachel a smile. "Sometimes it takes sandbox flowers a long time to grow."

Jenna snorts. "As in for*never*." She pulls out three squares of red tagboard and a box of craft sticks from her backpack. Then she pulls out a bag of noodles—rotini, elbow, wagon wheel, bow-tie—all dyed bright colors. She dumps everything onto the table, shifts to her knees, and holds up a wagon wheel. "I recommend using these," she tells us. "They stick best to picture frames."

Rachel grabs a glue bottle. "You can make anything stick if you use enough of this stuff." She twists open the cap.

"Glue away," Jenna snips, picking up a square of tagboard and another bottle of glue. "Just don't come crying to me when your frame turns into a noodle disaster." She dots glue along the edge of her tagboard and starts pressing craft sticks onto it, making a frame.

"I don't hardly ever come crying to you anymore," Rachel replies, pulling a piece of tagboard toward her. She plunks craft sticks and noodles around it and drizzles glue over them like icing.

At least Jenna and Rachel are talking to each other again. Ever since Rachel got mad at Jenna on Monday, she's only been talking to me. Yesterday, when I told her she could go first in hopscotch, she even said, "You're my big sister now, okay, Ida?"

I didn't know what to say, so I just kept drawing the "10" square at the top of our hopscotch path and pretended I hadn't heard her.

I snuck a look at Jenna, though. She was over by the porch, hunting for a perfect hopscotch rock, so maybe she didn't hear.

But she stiffened for a second, so maybe she did.

Since then, Jenna has been talking to Rachel again. Not all sweet, but not all spicy either.

Jenna keeps glancing up from her frame. She sighs loudly as Rachel adds another layer of noodles and glue to hers.

"If you ask me," Jenna finally says, "less is more when it comes to noodle frames."

"Then it's good nobody asked you," Rachel replies.

Jenna scowls at her sister. "Listen here, Rachel—"

"If you ask *me*," I interrupt, "this would be more fun if you two stopped fighting."

"We're not fighting," Jenna says. "We're talking."

"Then pick different words to talk with," I reply. "Because the ones you're using now are giving me a stomachache."

"She started it," Rachel grumbles.

"I didn't start anything," Jenna snaps.

I rub my stomach and go back to my frame. Rotini noodles twist down the sides of it like the new slides we're getting for our playground. Elbow macaroni and bowties bump along the top and bottom. All different colors.

"Finished," Jenna says, pushing back from the table. Wagon wheels circle her frame. Red, green, blue. Red, green, blue.

Jenna flicks glue snot off her fingers and gives my frame the once-over. "Not bad," she says. "For a first try."

"Thanks," I reply, squeezing in another rotini.

"What are you going to put inside it?" Jenna asks.

I look up. "Inside what? My frame?"

"Duh, yes."

"Duh, a picture."

"I know *that*. But which one?"

"Um . . . I don't know," I say. "I haven't given it much thought."

"You can have one of my school pictures," Rachel says, smiling at me.

"It's too late for that," Jenna says. "She's already getting one of mine."

"She is?" Rachel asks.

"I am?" I say.

Jenna nods at me. "And you can give me one of yours," she continues, "for *my* frame. That's what best friends do. Exchange pictures."

"Um . . . okay." That's what I say on the outside, but on the inside I'm saying, *Best friends? Me and Jenna?*

"Not mine though," Rachel says. "I'm saving my frame for a picture of my baby."

"How nice," Jenna says, glancing at Rachel. "More stuff for the baby's room." She looks at me again. "I'll bring the picture tomorrow, okay?"

"But it's Saturday tomorrow," I say. "You don't have to come over."

I don't say that last part in a mean way, but I guess that's how it sounds to Jenna. Her cheeks suddenly go red and her eyes get as narrow as the edges of spoons.

"Silly me," she says like her tongue is sticky with glue. She starts tossing noodles and craft sticks back into her bag.

"I didn't mean you couldn't—"

"I can't," Jenna cuts in. She takes a big breath and shakes back her braids. "Sorry," she says, "but I'll be too busy to come over tomorrow. I have to watch Miss Beanstalk plant jellybeans in our backyard. And help my dad change channels on the TV. Oh, *and* bring my mother snacks while she sits around waiting for Little Precious to be born."

She twists the lid closed on her glue bottle. Then she pulls a thimble out of a pocket in her backpack. "Come on," she says to us. "Game time. Hide the thimble."

# Chapter 5

Stacey's mom drops her off at my house on her way to work early the next morning. I haven't even eaten breakfast or changed out of my pajamas yet. Neither has Stacey.

"We should do a backwards day," I say as I help Stacey carry her stuff upstairs. "We'll start out with a slumber party and end with breakfast."

"Nice!" Stacey says.

"Roll out your sleeping bag," I say when we get to my room. "I'll go ask if we can have popcorn and soda instead of cereal and juice."

I find Dad in the kitchen, drinking a cup of coffee and reading *The Purdee Press*.

"Breakfast?" he asks, looking up from the newspaper.

"Actually, could we have our bedtime snack now and breakfast at, say, midnight?"

Dad's forehead wrinkles. Then it goes smooth. "Backwards day?" he asks.

"Yep," I say, digging chips and candy out of the snack cupboard.

"I'll make a batch of popcorn right after I finish reading this article about the spring carnival," he says.

"*Our* carnival? At school?" I pull two cans of soda out of the fridge and hug everything to my chest.

I look over Dad's shoulder. *Plans for School Auction/Carnival in Full Swing* tops the page. A photo of Mrs. Drews on a playground swing is under the headlines. She isn't actually swinging. She's just sitting there, gripping the chains and squinting at the camera. Maybe the sun is in her eyes. Or maybe she's sitting on one of her long braids. Or maybe she's feeling squished because the baby is taking up so much space inside her.

The caption under her picture says: *Paula Drews, PTA President and Chairperson of the spring fund-raiser.*

"There's a quote from Mrs. Drews too," Dad

says. *"Under my direction, this fund-raiser is sure to be Purdee's most successful event."*

"But she's not in charge anymore," I say. "Brooke's mom is."

Dad looks up. "They must have written the article before she stepped down."

I nod and wonder how Jenna will feel if she sees the article. Not great, I bet.

"Mrs. Morgan will make a good chairperson too," Dad says. "She knows how to make an event really shine."

I nod again. "Just like Brooke."

I think about Brooke. And Jenna. And how their talents fit together.

Jenna knows how to cook things up.

Brooke knows how to add the sprinkles.

I shift my snacks. "Popcorn?"

Dad sets down the newspaper. "I'm on it. Salty? Spicy? Sweet?" He pulls little jars of popcorn seasoning out of a cupboard.

"The works, please," I say. "Thank you. Good night!"

"Sleep tight!" he calls as I head upstairs in the bright morning sun.

Stacey is lying on her sleeping bag reading a girls' magazine. She gets a copy in the mail every couple of months, just like Brooke.

I dump the snacks on the floor and sit next to her. "Choco Chunks . . . cherry whips . . . dill pickle potato chips . . . root beer . . ." I say, looking over the pile of snacks. "Popcorn is on the way."

"Cherry whips, please," Stacey says, nibbling her fingernails and flipping magazine pages. "They're fan*tab*ulous."

I rip open the cherry whips bag. We tie knots in the long red strings and study the magazine.

"Ooo . . . look," Stacey says, tapping a picture of a very pretty girl wearing a sparkly brown dress. The shiny material ripples like a little stream running from her skinny shoulders to her knobby knees. "Brown is totally in."

"Is it?" I say.

Stacey nods and nibbles. "I've *got* to show this to Brooke. She'll think it's com*plete*ly smooth."

"Really?" I say, studying the dress. "It looks bumpy to me."

"Not *smooth* smooth," Stacey says, chewing. "Smooth as in really cute, you know?"

She blinks at me.

"Oh," I say, blinking back. I do a laugh. "I was just joking."

Stacey giggles. "You are hi*lar*ious, Ida."

I shrug and tie another knot in my whip.

Lately, Brooke and Stacey have been saying words that don't always make sense. Like they're learning a new language, only they keep forgetting to teach it to me.

Stacey flips to the end of the magazine and then tosses it aside. "Now what?" she asks, rolling over on her back. She pulls on her cherry whip until it snaps in two.

"A movie maybe?" I say. "How about that one about the girl who runs away from the evil orphanage and finds out she's really a princess. It's your favorite."

"*Was* my favorite," Stacey says back. She sits up, her eyes sparkling with another idea. "We could call someone. Only we'll disguise our voices, like Brooke and me did when we called Jolene that one time!"

"What did you say?" I ask, scooting in.

"We pretended to be Joey and Rusty. We go,

'Hey, Jolene, is your refrigerator running?'" She says it in a boy voice.

"Did Jolene fall for it?"

Stacey laughs. "Like an avalanche! She goes, 'Yes' and we go, 'Then you better hurry and catch it!' and hung up fast. Ohmygosh! We were in a complete state of hilarity!"

"Funny," I reply.

Stacey nods. "Who should we do it to this time? Meeka maybe? Or Randi?"

"How about Jenna?" I ask. "She could probably use a laugh."

"Jenna?" Stacey's eyes dim. "She'd call the prank police."

"No she wouldn't," I say. "She can be fun. Sometimes."

Stacey studies me for a moment. "What? Are you two best buds now?"

"Not *best* best." I fidget a little, remembering yesterday. When Jenna said I was her best friend. "But she's been coming over after school and it's not so bad. Not once you get used to her activity schedule. Besides, I think it's really boring at her house lately. Everyone is mostly just waiting for the baby to be born."

Stacey does a big sigh. "Fine," she says. "We can call Jenna. But later, okay? I can't take her this early in the morning."

"You mean this *late at night*," I say. "Remember? It's backwards day."

"Late, early, whatever," Stacey mumbles, and fishes another whip out of the bag. "I just can't take Jenna Drews."

We grab the snacks and head downstairs.

After the movie I call Jenna.

But no one answers.

Her family must have decided to do something fun today after all.

By noon we make it normal day again. Mostly because it's hard to remember to keep saying things like, "Aren't the stars lovely tonight?" and "What a day! I'm dying for a bubble bath" when the sun is shining and the birds are singing like crazy in the trees.

We get dressed and I try calling Jenna again, but there's still no answer, so I give up and let Stacey call Brooke.

They talk for a long time.

When Stacey finally clicks off the phone she

says, "Brooke's going to meet us at the park!"

"Brooke?" I say. "At the park? But she hates it there."

"She likes it when I'm there," Stacey replies. "I mean, when *we're* there."

Stacey jumps up and starts shoveling markers back into a bucket that's sitting on my kitchen table. We've been designing clothes for the stars. It's one of Stacey's favorite things to do now. Sparkly dresses. Feathery scarves. High heels. She's good at drawing all their accessories. I'm better at doing their faces and pet Chihuahuas.

"We could take the shortcut through the woods," I say when we come to the corner that turns toward Jenna's house. "Jenna won't care and, besides, nobody's home."

"Sounds good to me," Stacey replies.

Jenna's garage door is open when we get there, but only one car is inside. We walk up the steps to the front door and ring the bell.

No one answers. Except Biscuit.

*"Yipyipyip!"*

I can see his jumpy little shadow through the foggy door window.

Then something else catches my eye.

A doll wearing a paper towel diaper is leaning against the porch railing.

"This must be Rachel's," I say, stooping down and picking up the doll. "Why would she go away and leave it outside?"

"Because she's a kid?" Stacey replies.

I try peeking through the door's window again, but I can't see anything clearly. Then I put my ear against it. "Listen . . ."

Stacey leans in.

Biscuit is still yipping, but I can hear another sound too. A TV commercial.

"Weird," I say. "They would never leave without turning off the TV."

"We forget to turn stuff off all the time," Stacey says. "Radio. Lights. TV."

"The Drewses don't," I say, stepping back. "They keep a checklist by the door."

Stacey shrugs. "Maybe they were in a hurry. C'mon, let's go before Brooke gives up on us."

Stacey takes off around the house. I set the

doll on the doorstep and follow along.

Stacey hurries down the path through Jenna's woods. She doesn't stop when we cross the spot where the crooked path starts.

But I do.

I'd really like to know what's down that path besides wind chimes. But I know Stacey is in a hurry to see Brooke. And besides, it doesn't feel right to go down that path without Jenna.

I run toward the park.

"I called the others," Brooke says when we get there. "Randi, Meeka, Jolene—"

"Jenna?" I ask.

"Not her," Brooke says. "She's not in my circle."

"Neither are the others," I say. "Just Rusty and Joey."

As soon as I say it I realize my mistake. But it's too late.

Brooke gives me a blank look. "My *calling* circle. Not my *friendless* circle." She turns to Stacey. "What did she think?"

Stacey laughs. "Ida was just joking." She looks at me. "Right?"

I nod. "Ha-ha."

Brooke studies me like I just stepped off a flight from another planet. Then she zeroes in on Stacey. "Everyone was busy or gone or whatever, so you know what that means . . ." She gives Stacey's arm a squeeze. "More swings for us!"

Brooke grabs Stacey's hand. Stacey grabs mine.

We crack the whip all the way to the swings, laughing and screaming like we are the best friends in the world.

Well, Stacey and Brooke do.

I mostly just hang on and try not to get whipped into a tree.

I wonder if they'd notice if I did.

# Chapter

# 6

"Where were you on Saturday?" I ask Jenna when I get to the bus stop on Monday morning. "I tried calling, but no one answered."

"Let's see . . ." Jenna says, tapping her chin and pretending to think hard. "Where was I? Oh, yes. I remember. I was at the hospital."

"The hospital?" I glance around for Rachel, but she's not there. "Did something happen to your sister?"

Jenna gives me a squint. "No, nothing happened to *her*. Something happened to *me*. I practically *died* of boredom. My mom started having contractions, so we had to take her to the ER. That stands for *emergency room*."

"I know that," I say. "I watch TV. But . . . contractions?"

Jenna nods. "You know, cramps? Because of the baby. They hooked her up to machines and gave her medicine until the contractions stopped. Which. Took. *All*. *Day*. Practically. My dad wouldn't leave her, so me and Rachel had to sit and watch cartoons on a barely hearable TV and do coloring books that some other kid had already scribbled to death."

"Oh."

Jenna pauses. "So that's what I was doing while you and Stacey were having fun, fun, fun."

"It wasn't all fun," I say.

Jenna's jaw twitches. "It wasn't?"

I shake my head. "It was partly fun and partly Brooke."

"Brooke?"

I nod. "We met up at the park. At first it was okay, but then Brooke got the ginormous idea—that's her new favorite word, by the way, *ginormous*—that we should camp out at her house."

Jenna's chin drops. "*Brooke* wanted to *camp out*?"

"Uh-huh," I say. "Saturday night. Only she didn't have any actual camping gear, except for a flashlight with no batteries. So we roasted cocktail wieners over candles. And made s'mores in the microwave. Which was actually fun, but then we had to sleep on the patio in her old portable playhouse. Only I didn't sleep much because the playhouse was built for two, so I had about one inch of room. Plus, Brooke and Stacey talked all night. I talked a little too, but mostly I just stayed still and tried not to use up all the oxygen."

Jenna snorts a laugh.

"Ha-ha, thanks," I say, frowning. "So see? You're not the only one who had a not-so-fun weekend."

"Okay, okay," Jenna says. "I get it."

I swallow to soften my voice. "Is your mom okay? And the baby? And where's Rachel?"

Jenna brushes back her braids. "My mother is fine, Little Precious is fine, and Rachel is fine. She gets to sleep in this morning because of our *ginormous* weekend. My dad's driving her to school on his lunch break."

"Not you?"

Jenna shakes her head. "No, my parents think I'm old enough to handle a family crisis and still go to school on time."

Quinn and his sister, Tess, arrive just as the bus comes around the corner.

We all pile on.

I sit next to Jenna. We work the word *ginormous* into our conversation as much as possible.

*I wonder how I did on that ginormous math test last Friday . . .*

*I bet I got a ginormous A . . .*

*Look at that crazy dog with the ginormous head . . .*

*It probably has a ginormous case of rabies . . .*

*Brooke found a spider in the portable playhouse and had a ginormous fit . . .*

*What a ginormous surprise . . .*

By the time our bus pulls up to the school, we both have ginormous laugh-aches.

"What's so ha-ha?" Brooke asks when me and Jenna get to the coatroom. All the other girls are there too—Stacey, Randi, Meeka, and Jolene.

"Oh, nothing," Jenna says, hanging her backpack on a coat hook and wiping laugh tears from her eyes. Her face is so red it makes her blond hair look spaghetti white. "Ida just told a . . . *ginormous* joke."

She says it just like Brooke would. I hug my stomach and laugh, only no sound comes out.

Brooke crinkles her eyebrows and chews her gum. "Let's hear it," she says to me.

"Wha . . . wha . . . what?" I reply.

"Duh," Brooke says. "The ginormous joke."

Jenna hugs her stomach too. She grabs a coat hook to steady herself.

"Um . . ." I say, glancing at Jenna. "Um . . ."

Jenna flutters a hand at me. "Go on, Ida," she says, sniffling back snot. "Tell Brooke what we're laughing about."

Jenna does a sly smile. She's probably getting back at me for putting her on the spot with Tom the other day. Jenna always likes to even the score.

"Joke . . . joke . . . joke . . ." Randi chants.

Everyone nudges in.

I shoot another look at Jenna and try to think fast. "Um . . . Knock, knock?"

Brooke rolls her eyes and snaps her gum.

"Who's there?" Stacey asks.

I glance around, trying to think of who could be at the door. A coat hook? Cargo pants? Raspberry mint bubble gum? Sparkly sneakers?

"We haven't got all day," Brooke says. "Do you have a joke or don't you?"

I watch Brooke chew and chomp like the cows that live on Dylan Anderson's farm.

A joke pops into my brain.

"Knock, knock," I say again.

"Who's there?" Brooke replies.

"Cows go," I say.

"Cows go who?" everyone chimes in.

I shake my head. "No, they don't. Cows go *moo*. Owls go *who*."

I do a clever smile.

Brooke frowns. "*That's* what you two were spazzing over?"

I shrug. "Mostly."

Brooke swallows her gum and grabs Stacey's arm. She pulls her into our classroom.

Meeka, Jolene, and Randi follow along.

Jenna gives me a smile.


"Thank goodness *I* don't have to wear a crepe-paper mouse nest," Brooke says as we gather in the pigpen for Jenna's last playground ceremony. Today we say good-bye to the bouncy horse and seal.

Brooke adjusts the sparkly tiara on her head. She brought it from home. She has a whole collection from all the pageants she's been in.

"Good," Jenna snips back. "I didn't have time to make Randi a new crown, so now she can wear yours."

Jenna steps past Brooke and holds a crepe-paper crown out to Randi.

"Gee," Randi says. "Thanks." She plops the crown on her head.

Jenna hands crowns to Meeka and Jolene.

"And you can't force me to do that goofy step-step-turn thing," Brooke continues. "Honestly, Jenna, it looks like something a kindergartener would do."

"No one is forcing you to do anything," Jenna says back to Brooke. She hands a crown to Stacey and one to me. "No one is even forcing you to *stay*. If you want to leave the group, then leave the group."

Brooke huffs. Her tiara tilts. "*Leave* the group? I *am* the group, Jenna. If I go, I'm taking the others with me."

Meeka and Jolene trade glances.

Stacey stiffens.

"Lighten up, Brooke," Randi says, brushing back a crepe-paper streamer. "Let's get this done. I've got a basketball game to win."

Jenna puts the last crown on her head. "Line up behind me," she tells us. "Remember, step-step-*twirl*. Step-step-*twirl*. All the way across the playground. Then ten bounces each. Five on the horse. Five on the seal. I'll bounce first."

Randi gets in line behind Jenna.

I step behind Randi and look back at the others.

Brooke crosses her arms. "No," she says. "I won't." She looks at Stacey, Meeka, and Jolene. "Stick with me and you'll never have to wear crepe paper again."

Meeka studies the streamers dangling in front of her eyes.

Then she steps closer to Brooke.

So does Jolene.

They take off their crowns and let them fall to the ground.

I look at Stacey.

She bites her lip.

And lets her crown fall too.

Brooke smiles.

Jenna squints. "You've made your choice," she says to them. "You're on your own now."

"No, *you* are," Brooke says back. She links arms with Stacey. Stacey links up with Meeka. Meeka links up with Jolene.

I look at them and shake my head. *"Dumb."*

Stacey narrows her eyes at me. "Who are you calling *dumb*, Ida?" Her voice sounds like she's sucking on ice.

"I'm not calling anyone dumb," I reply. "I'm saying *this* is dumb." I glance around at everyone. "Splitting up the group. Over what? Crepe-paper crowns?"

"It's over a lot more than that," Brooke snaps. She shoots a look at Jenna. Then she shoots another look at me and Randi. "I hope you two don't mind getting *pushed* around. Because that's what you're in for. If you stick with *her*." She zaps Jenna again.

"I'm not the only *pushy* one around here," Jenna tells her. She turns to me and Randi. "C'mon," she says. "We don't need them."

Jenna step-step-twirls out of the pigpen.

Randi follows along.

"Last chance, Ida," Brooke says, tapping her toe on the green grass. "Stay with us *winners* or go with those *losers.*"

I study Brooke for a moment.

And Meeka.

And Jolene.

And Stacey.

"Everyone's losing, if you ask me," I say.

Then I step-step-twirl away.

When we get back to our classroom after recess it's covered with stuff. A white sheet of paper is on each of our desks and a mound of colored fabric is piled on the reading table.

"First, trace around each other's hands on practice paper," Mrs. Eddy tells us. "Carefully and neatly. Then cut out your handprints with equal care and neatness. When I'm satisfied you've done a good job with paper, you'll move on to cloth."

Jenna's hand shoots up. "But you said we're making a *tree* quilt, not a handprint quilt."

"We are," Mrs. Eddy says. "Didn't I tell you? Your handprints will be the leaves on the tree."

Mrs. Eddy unfolds a piece of fabric. It's almost as big as she is. A tree trunk is sewn to the front of it. Not a real one. A cloth one. Bare branches spread out from it like spider legs.

"No offense," Brooke says, waving her hand to get Mrs. Eddy's attention. "But your tree looks dead."

"*Your* tree," Mrs. Eddy corrects her. "It belongs to all of you now. And it won't look dead after you fill its branches with your colorful handprints."

"The leaves," Meeka says.

"That's right," Mrs. Eddy replies. "You'll stitch around them and use fabric markers and paint pens to write friendship words on them before I sew everything to the tree. Now, let's get started. Choose a partner to trace your handprint."

Stacey glances at me. Then she scoots her chair closer to Dominic and starts helping him.

I can't believe she picked a boy over me. But I guess anything can happen when you're fighting with your best friend.

I trace Jenna's hand.

She traces mine.

A few careful cuts later and we're showing them to Mrs. Eddy.

"Good work," she says to me and Jenna. "You're ready to choose your cloth. Look for colors and patterns that express who you are."

"Pass the purple please," I hear Brooke say as we sit down at the reading table. Other kids are already there too, digging through the pile of fabric. "All of it. I'm a purple*holic*!"

Joey snatches up a square of bright purple cloth and hands it to Brooke. "Here you go, Brookey!"

Brooke gives Joey a squint. But she takes the cloth.

"Joey, tell Ida to pass you that square so you can pass it to me," Stacey says. "The one with the purple polka dots. I'm a purpleholic too!" She points to a piece of fabric that's lying right in front of me.

Joey glances away from Brooke. "Tell her yourself," he says to Stacey.

Stacey huffs and turns to Tom. He's sitting across the table from me. "Tom, will you please pass me that purple polka-dot square?"

Tom glances from the square to me to Stacey. "I could," he says. "But Ida's closer. It makes more sense to ask her."

Stacey does a bigger huff. *"Boys,"* she says. Then she leans across the table, reaching for the polka dots.

Jenna flicks them away.

Stacey scowls.

Jenna smiles.

I sigh.

And grab the cloth.

I hold it out to Stacey. "Here," I say to her.

Brooke looks up.

Stacey reaches for the cloth.

But then she catches Brooke's eye and stops.

She snatches a different square instead.

Blue with orange stripes.

Not her favorite colors. Or pattern.

Stacey sits down.

I jerk my hand back like I touched something hot. And stare at the polka dots I'm still holding. *Just like Jenna said in the pigpen,* I think to myself. *Stacey's made her choice. And it's not me. It's Brooke.*

The polka dots run together like they're growing purple fur. I blink away my tears before looking at Stacey again.

But she's gone.

Marching with Brooke to their desks. Waving their fabric like they're leading a parade.

Other kids fill in. Reaching. Looking. Tossing.

"Dibs on skeletons," Zane says, pushing butterflies and kittens aside.

"Dibs on race cars," Quinn says, reaching past Zane.

"Dibs on skeletons *driving* race cars," Randi says, reaching past both of them.

A piece of fabric falls in front of me. It's purple, but not polka-dot purple. Flowers are scattered across it. Pink with yellow centers.

I wipe my eyes and look at Jenna. She's sitting next to me. "Did you drop this?" I ask, setting down the polka dots and picking up the flowers.

"Yes," Jenna replies. "On purpose."

"No wonder," Joey says, holding his nose. "Flowers. *Pee-u!*"

Zane nods. "Stinky pinky!"

Quinn laughs. "Make mine a Twinkie!"

The boys howl. It doesn't take much to get them going.

"You guys are nuts," Randi says. "Flowers are quiet and cute. Just like Ida." She looks at the cloth and gives me a thumbs-up. "It's you."

I sniffle and give her a smile.

Quinn stops laughing and studies the square of race cars in his hand. "Quiet and cute," he mumbles.

Then he glances at me. And takes off for his desk.

Jenna gives me a nudge.

"What?" I whisper.

"You know what," she whispers back. "Quiet and *cute*? He wasn't talking about race cars."

I fidget a little and glance toward Stacey, trying to catch her eye. Trying to see if there is any sadness in them.

But she's huddled up with Brooke, tracing her purple handprint.

I tuck my flowers on my lap.

"Score!" Zane shouts, pulling a piece of black cloth out of the pile. It's sprinkled with skulls. He flutters it like a dainty hankie. "Later, ladies!" he says to all of us, even the boys, and gallops back to his desk.

"I'll help you find one," I tell Jenna.

"Not pink," she replies. "Or blue. No teddy bears. No duckies. No pacifiers."

"How about this one?" Tom holds up a green square with yellow bees buzzing across it. "Green, because you love nature."

"And bees," Randi says. "Because they sting." She grins.

"They also make honey," Tom continues. "And they work hard to keep the hive together."

I think about our group and how it's falling apart. None of us, not even Jenna, have been very good bees lately.

Still, I take the cloth from Tom and pass it to her. "You?" I ask.

Jenna takes it. "Me."

# Chapter

# 7

"I have an idea," I say when me and Jenna get to my house after school on Thursday. Rachel already ran inside.

"What?" Jenna asks, sitting on my porch steps and digging two mini boxes of raisins out of her backpack. I sit next to her and she hands one to me.

"We could take a break from your schedule, just for today, and go to the Purdee Good," I say. "Me and Stacey used to meet there every Thursday after she was done with dance class. We'd split a giant cookie and draw pictures on the paper placemats and talk about stuff. School. Homework. Which boys were annoying us the most. Plus, I heard Stacey tell Brooke they got new ice cream flavors this week. Double Trouble

Fudge. Coconut Caramel. Blue Moon. We could eat our treats there and then run home quick with a cone for Rachel."

Jenna opens her box and pinches up a raisin. "Why would we want to do all that?"

I shrug. "For fun."

There hasn't been a lot of fun going on this week with everyone fighting. Meeka and Jolene won't talk to me. Stacey will barely even look at me. If I walk into the girls' bathroom while they're in there, Brooke shouts, "Red alert!" and then marches everyone out. Same goes for the playground. If I sit by them at lunch, they gather up their trays and Brooke leads them to a different table. If I pass them worksheets during class, they shake them off like they're crawling with germs.

Ida germs.

Jenna and Randi get the same treatment. But I don't think it bothers them as much as it bothers me.

And tomorrow will be even worse. Because of our class trip to the Laura Ingalls Wilder Museum and cabin. Everyone will be squished inside a school bus for the drive over. And then the chaperones will make us stay in a group while we're there. I wouldn't be surprised if Brooke brings along the jug of hand sanitizer Mr. Crow keeps in our classroom so she can rub some on every time she has to be by me.

I don't want to be treated like I'm contagious.

And I don't want to treat other people like they are too.

Fighting isn't one of my talents.

"I don't have any money for ice cream," Jenna says. "And besides, *they* will probably be there."

I know who Jenna means by *they*. Stacey, Brooke, Meeka, and Jolene.

"We could stop at your house and get some money from your mom. And if *they* are there, we'll just go in, buy our stuff, and run away again."

Jenna frowns. "I don't *have* extra money for treats, okay? Not since my mom had to quit everything, including her job, because of the baby. And I *don't* run away from Brooke Morgan. Ever."

I'm quiet for a moment. "I've got some allowance money left over. I'll buy. And besides, isn't *running* away from Brooke the same as *staying* away?"

Jenna shakes her head. "I don't want your allowance. And if you *run* away from the person you're fighting with, she wins. If you *stay* away, nobody wins. Get it?"

I sigh and shake my head. "Not really. If I got to choose between fighting with someone and being friends with her again, I'd choose being friends. Even if the person I was fighting with was Brooke Morgan."

Jenna huffs. "You *are* fighting with her, remember? And you wouldn't stop if she said bad things about *your* family."

"What bad things?"

Jenna looks away. "Just . . . things. Bad things. She deserved to get shoved."

"You shoved her?"

Jenna chews a raisin. "*Barely.* But she acted like I ran her over with a truck."

"Did you tell her you were sorry?"

"Of course not," Jenna replies. She crumples her raisin box. "If people say bad things about my family, they don't deserve an apology. I plan to stay mad at her forever."

I nibble a raisin and think about how far away forever is. And how old I'll be when I get there. Older than my grandma May. Even older than Mrs. Eddy. And how hard it would be to stay mad at someone for that many years. And how much better it would be if people stopped trying to fight forever and started trying to be *friends* forever instead.

Jenna tosses her raisin box over my porch railing. "Just forget I said anything about not having enough money for treats, okay? *Don't* go blabbing it around. All I need is for Brooke to hear. There's nothing she likes better than bragging about how much more money she has than everyone else."

I give Jenna a frown. "I *don't* blab," I say, throwing down my raisin box. "And I *don't* like raisins. I've never eaten dead flies, but I don't think it would be much different."

I cross my arms and glare across the street at Mr. Juhl's front yard. Green grass polka-dotted with yellow dandelions. Like one square in a giant quilt.

A bee buzzes by. I glance at Jenna. Why do I

put up with her? Like Stacey said, she can be hard to take. But if I didn't take her, who would?

Jenna shoos the bee away and glances back. "Okay, I'm sorry," she says. "Don't be mad at me. I know you're not a blabber. Things have just been a little . . . messed up lately. At my house. Because of the baby."

Jenna picks up my raisin box and fiddles with the lid.

"Me too," I say, taking the box from her. "I'm sorry for getting mad."

I pop a raisin into my mouth. "Yum," I say. "What else is on today's schedule?"

Jenna reaches inside her backpack and pulls out a clump of embroidery thread. Red. Green. Yellow. Blue.

"Friendship bracelets," she says. "I'll make one for you, and you make one for me. Then we'll both make one for Randi. *All* matching. That'll show *them*."

"Fun," I reply.

"Just so you know," I say to Mom as we pull into the school parking lot on Friday morning.

"This is probably going to be a long, boring day."

Mom is driving me to school because she volunteered to go along on our class trip. Jenna's mom was supposed to be one of the chaperones, but because she has to stay home and rest until the baby is born, my mom is substituting for her.

"It'll be whatever kind of day you make it be, Ida," Mom replies.

I sigh. "You're not going to say stuff like that to the other kids, are you?"

Mom does a shocked look. "What? No sage advice? No pep talks? No hilarious jokes?"

"Nope, nope, and *pleeease* nope," I say. "You are only allowed to talk to the other parents. And Mr. Crow. And me, a little. *Quietly*. Don't do that big tuba laugh."

"Ha!" Mom laughs. She grins. "Like that?"

"That's the one," I say, and slide out of the car.

I hurry ahead of Mom to my classroom. Everyone is already there. I see Stacey, Brooke, and Meeka gathered around Jolene's desk, comparing snacks they brought along for the bus ride. I start heading over to them, but then I remember we're fighting, so I stop. Jenna steps in front of me. She's my buddy for the day.

"Here," she says, holding up a big piece of bright red tagboard that's bent and stapled into the shape of a wide cone. "I made us sun bonnets like Laura and Mary Ingalls used to wear."

Jenna pushes the tagboard bonnet into my hands and puts a matching one on her head. "I'll be Laura," she says, tying two strands of yellow yarn under her chin. "You can be Mary. Only not *blind* Mary. I don't want to have to lead you around all day."

I blink at my bonnet. "Are the other girls wearing them?"

"Doubt it," Jenna says, glancing across the room. "If we get lost in the Big Woods the search-and-rescue team will spot us immediately. Too bad for them."

"I don't think the Big Woods are so big anymore," I say. "Mr. Crow says it's more like the Big Cornfield now."

Jenna takes my bonnet and puts it on my head. "I once heard about a kid who got lost in a cornfield." She tugs on the yarn and ties a double knot under my chin. "If it hadn't been for his red base-ball cap he would have been a goner."

I don't really want to wear a bright red tag-board bonnet all day. But Jenna seems so excited about them and she hasn't had a lot to be excited about lately, so I sigh and do a little step turn. "How do I look?" I ask.

Jenna gives me the once-over. "Noticeable," she says. "Sensible. Like a real pioneer." Jenna picks up a third bonnet and looks around the room. "I made one for Randi too."

Randi is talking with Rusty and Joey in their friendless circle. Brooke prances up to them and pulls four tiaras out of a bag that's on her desk. She puts the biggest one on her head and then gives the others to Stacey, Meeka, and Jolene.

I scratch at the yarn that's tied around my neck and stare at their four sparkly heads, all huddled together in a circle. Whispering. Glancing. Giggling.

Jenna marches over to Randi with the extra tagboard bonnet. Randi takes it, folds it, and stuffs it into the back pocket of her jeans.

Jenna gives Randi a frown. She says something I can't hear and then turns sharply away.

The four sparkly heads dart up as Jenna marches past them. They stare as she steps up to me and straightens my bonnet. Then they huddle even closer and giggle even harder.

Jenna asks me something, but I don't really hear because my ears are pounding from all that giggling. My heart is pounding too. So hard it hurts my chest.

Mr. Crow walks in from the hallway wearing a white shirt, blue jeans, and red suspenders. His long hair is braided down his back and a cowboy hat is on his head. He pulls a wooden whistle out of his shirt pocket and blows into it. It sounds just like a train. "*Alllll* aboard!" he calls.

Everyone charges toward him.

Toward us.

Quinn bumps into me. I bump into Jenna. Jenna bumps into Mr. Crow.

I hear something crumple.

"Hey!" Jenna snaps at Quinn. "You dented my bonnet!"

"It wasn't me," Quinn says. He glances behind him. "It was Zaney."

"Nu-uh," Zane says. "It was Dilly Bar." He pokes his thumb at one of the Dylans.

"It was *all* of you idiots!" Jenna shouts. "Thanks for ruining my day!"

"Jenna," Mr. Crow says. "Name calling is not on today's schedule."

Jenna ducks her chin.

"What do you say to the boys?" Mr. Crow asks her.

"Sorry," Jenna mumbles.

Mr. Crow nods and walks down the line, counting heads.

I swallow my tears, reach up and flatten Jenna's brim. "It's rough being a pioneer," I say to her.

"Hmph," Jenna grunts. She crosses her arms and faces forward again. "It's rougher being me."

I glance back toward Stacey, but I notice Quinn watching me.

*Studying* me.

I squint at him from under my bright red brim. *"What?"* I say.

"Nothing," he says back. "It's just . . . you look like . . . a tulip."

98

I squint harder. "Thanks a lot." I'm not in the mood for boys today.

Quinn's face goes all innocent. "Not in a bad way," he says.

"How can it *not* be bad to look like a tulip?"

Quinn shrugs. "They're . . . pretty. And they don't stink."

A little lever drops behind my belly button. Like on a toaster. A moment later my face heats up.

No boy has ever told me I don't stink before.

Especially not one I secretly like.

I turn away quickly before Quinn can see that my cheeks and my sun bonnet match.

Mr. Crow blows his train whistle again and waves us down the hallway.

Four tiaras bounce and sparkle.

Jenna yanks my arm.

We're on our way.

# Chapter

# 8

There's one good thing about being Jenna's buddy on a class trip. She's an expert at pushing and shoving her way to the best seat on the bus.

We tumble into the very back one. Stacey and Brooke are right in front of us. Quinn and Tom are in front of them. Meeka, Jolene, and Randi are across the aisle. Randi is sitting with Rusty, but for now she's turned around on her knees, facing the rest of us girls. I guess Randi has forgotten that she's supposed to be fighting with half of them. Or maybe she just doesn't care. Randi doesn't like to choose sides, unless it's for basketball.

The chaperones get settled in the front seats while Mr. Crow counts heads again. Then he gives the bus driver a thumbs-up.

The driver closes the door and the bus pulls away from the school.

Jenna unzips her lunch box and slips out an egg salad sandwich. She peels back the waxed paper it's wrapped in and takes a bite.

"You didn't have to bring a lunch, you know," I say. "The chaperones are doing a picnic. Hot dogs. Chips. Punch. My mom made a hundred brownies. She said Mr. Crow is even grilling burgers that are made from *real* buffalos. No lie."

Jenna tucks one of her braids behind her bonnet and takes another bite of her sandwich. "This isn't my lunch," she says. "It's my bus snack. And I don't *do* buffalo. Or junk food."

"Really?" I say, sliding her a look. "That's interesting, because the last time we went to the mall you ate half of my cheesy pretzel and fifteen of my French fries."

Jenna squints, sucking egg salad from her teeth. "You *counted* the French fries?"

I nod. "Fifteen. Plus three slurps of my very berry icy."

Jenna takes another bite of her sandwich. "Well, it's not like I *bought* that junk."

"Want some?" I hear someone say.

I push back my bonnet and see a smile.

A Stacey smile. Bright and sparkly, just like the tiara on her head.

She leans over the back of her seat and dances a bag of cheese puffs in front of me.

"Thanks," I say, reaching toward the bag.

Stacey pulls it away. "On one condition," she says. "You and Jenna have to switch seats with Brooke and me. Okay?" She does the smile bigger.

My hand freezes. I look at Jenna.

"No way," Jenna says, taking another bite of her sandwich.

I look at Stacey again. "I guess not."

The sparkle slips from her smile. She narrows her eyes. "Then I guess not too," she says, popping a cheese puff into her mouth and plopping down next to Brooke again.

"I told you it wouldn't work," I hear Brooke say. "She's Jenna's little puppet now."

My face gets red hot again, but for a totally different reason. *How could she do her sparkly smile on me?*

"Me, me, me!" Randi shouts, bouncing on her

knees and eyeing Stacey's bag of cheese puffs. She tilts her head back and opens her mouth.

Stacey shoots.

She scores.

Randi claps her hands and barks like a seal.

Stacey lets another puff fly.

More barks.

More puffs.

They keep it up until the bus driver hollers.

Randi sits down.

Jenna rolls her eyes. She winds a piece of dental floss around her fingers and jabs it between her teeth. "Cheese puffs aren't made with real cheese, you know," she says loudly. "Look at the package. Real cheese *flavor.* That's not the same thing."

Brooke snorts and shakes her head. Her tiara tilts.

Randi barks again and Stacey takes aim with another puff. It's trickier now that Randi is sitting.

The puff bounces off her nose and lands in the aisle.

Rusty leans across Randi, eyeing the puff.

"One one thousand, two one thousand, three one thousand . . ." he counts.

Quinn snatches up the puff and pops it into his mouth.

"Ew," Brooke says, sucking puff dust off her fingers. "Dis*gust*ing."

Jenna leans forward. "You just ate a gazillion germs!" she shouts past Brooke to Quinn.

Quinn looks at Jenna and smacks his lips. "Tasty!"

"Thank you, Florence Nightingale," Brooke snips, batting at Jenna's bonnet. "You can go back to your prairie now."

Jenna squints to Brooke. "Florence Nightingale wasn't a pioneer. She was a nurse during the Civil War."

"Crimean War, actually," Tom says, glancing back at Jenna.

Jenna shoots a look at Tom. "Thank you, Albert Einstein."

"What*ev*er," Brooke says. "I just don't think we should be taking medical advice from someone with tagboard tied to her head."

Stacey snorts.

"Besides, Jenna," Tom adds, twisting all the way around. "Ten-second rule."

"Yep," Randi chimes in. "Quinn got to the puff in three. So no germs."

Meeka and Jolene nod.

Jenna sits back hard and tosses her floss onto the floor. "Idiots," she grumbles.

I sit back too and wish I had thought to bring along my own bag of cheese puffs. They would fill up the empty spot in my stomach that got left behind when Stacey took her bag away.

Jenna pulls out a pencil and a puzzle book and starts rearranging jumbled letters to make words.

Randi and Rusty huddle over a handheld.

Meeka and Jolene sing pioneer songs.

Brooke and Stacey stick yellow Starbursts between their teeth and talk like pirates to Tom and Quinn.

I watch Stacey's tiara bounce as she laughs and butt hops with Brooke.

*Did she think I'd actually fall for that smile? She knows me better than that. I'm not stupid. I'm not a puppet. I'm her BFF.*

I look out my window and watch cars and cows and trees zip by. "At least I used to be," I say.

"Let's go over a few rules," Mr. Crow says when we arrive at the Laura Ingalls Wilder Museum.

Jenna sits up. She's a big fan of rules.

"No pushing, no shoving, no shouting." Mr. Crow counts off on his fingers.

"Same old, same old," Brooke mumbles.

"Buddies stick together," he continues, "in the museum and on our walk to Lake Pepin afterward."

Jenna grabs my hand.

"I don't think he means *glued* together," I whisper, squirming my hand like a little fish caught in a net.

Jenna squeezes tighter. "Better safe than sorry."

The museum is small, so it doesn't take us very long to look at everything: old farm tools. Furniture. Pioneer clothes. Real sun bonnets made out of cloth, not tagboard. We gather around a glass display case. The museum lady shows us old photographs of Laura and her family. Then she takes out a copy of a letter that Laura wrote to some schoolchildren after she grew up and became a famous author.

"Major antique," Tom whispers. "Totally unique."

"You said it," Jenna whispers back.

I see a smile pass between them.

*"Dear Children,"* the museum lady reads from the letter, *"I was born in the 'Little House in the Big Woods' of Wisconsin on February 7 in the year 1867. I lived everything that happened in my books. It was a long story, filled with sunshine and shadows . . ."*

Brooke flips open the top on a ring she's wearing and dabs at the lip gloss inside. She runs her finger over her lips. Then she nudges Stacey and glances at the museum lady. *"Borrring,"* she whispers, and holds the ring out to Stacey.

Stacey dabs the gloss.

I can smell the strawberries from over here.

*". . . Today our way of living and our schools are much different; so many things have made living and learning easier. But the real things haven't changed . . ."*

The museum lady pauses and looks at us over the top of her glasses like Mr. Crow does when he wants to make sure we're all paying attention. Her eyes land on Brooke and stay there until everyone else is looking at Brooke too.

Stacey gives Brooke a nudge.

Brooke glances up from whispering to Meeka.

"Oops," Brooke says, snapping her ring shut and giving the museum lady a sweet strawberry smile.

The museum lady clears her throat and starts reading again. *"But the real things haven't changed. It is still best to be honest and truthful; to make the most of what we have; to be happy with simple pleasures and to be cheerful and have courage when things go wrong."*

She looks right at me when she reads that last part. *Have courage when things go wrong.* I glance around at the other girls and think about how wrong things have been between us lately. All because Brooke and Jenna are too stubborn to apologize and be friends again.

Then I look at Stacey. I know I should talk to her. But sometimes it's hard to do the things you know you should do.

"That's all she wrote," the museum lady says, placing the letter back in the display case.

"Hurray," Brooke says, straightening her tiara. She grabs Stacey's arm and pulls her away.

"That was hardly boring at all!" Stacey says as we leave the museum and get ready to cross a busy road on our way to Lake Pepin. Mr. Crow put my mom and Jolene's mom in charge of us girls, which means we have to stay in a group so no one gets run over.

At first, we try to keep an invisible dividing line between us—me, Jenna, and Randi on one side; Stacey, Brooke, Meeka, and Jolene on the other—but the line gets tangled up in our sandals and sneakers as we tear across the road. Then it seems to disappear completely as we trip and scream-laugh down a steep hill that leads to the lake. By the time we reach the bottom, we're so jumbled together you can hardly tell we're fighting at all.

"Did you see that quilt at the museum?" Jolene asks, breathless from running. "The one with all the names sewn on it?"

Meeka nods, untangling her hair from her tiara. "An old-fashioned friendship quilt, just like Mrs. Eddy told us about."

"I'm just glad to finally be out of there," Brooke says, throwing back her arms and knocking my tagboard bonnet off my head. It dangles down my back. Brooke's crown glitters in the sun. "I need my space."

"Looks like you need mine too," I mumble, putting my bonnet back on my head.

"Whoa, big lake," Randi says as we step onto the rocky beach of Lake Pepin. A truck with a boat trailer rumbles past us. People laugh and shout from the docks that stretch like giant fingers into the choppy water.

Jenna huffs. "Lake Superior is way bigger. My family goes there every summer."

"Lake Superior is a *bathtub* compared to the ocean," Brooke sasses back. "Has your *family* been to the ocean, Jenna?" She does quote marks with her fingers when she says the word *family*. Then she smiles sweetly. "*My* family has. Tons of times."

Jenna gives Brooke a scowl and turns away.

We scramble around on the beach for a while. Rock skipping. Stick throwing. Bug poking. I think about Laura and Mary coming here when they were little. And how they threw rocks into Lake Pepin just like we are. I bet they thought it looked big too.

"How about a picture, girls?" Mom asks, walking up to us with her camera.

"I thought you'd never ask," Brooke says, draping her arms around Stacey's neck like they're posing for the cover of a magazine.

Mom clicks a few shots. Stacey and Brooke. Meeka and Jolene. Me and Jenna. Randi and Rusty. Then she gets us all huddled together.

"Girls *only*," Brooke says, shoving Rusty away.

Rusty stumbles back. "But Brookey," he says, all pouty. "You're breaking my heart!"

"I'll break your *nose* if you don't go away," Brooke says, giving Rusty another shove.

"Surprise, surprise," I hear Jenna mumble.

We smile at the camera.

The boys make faces behind us.

"Good one," Mom says, looking up. "You girls make such a cute group of friends."

We fidget and glance at each other, remembering that we're not supposed to be friends. Cute or otherwise. We're supposed to be fighting.

Stacey, Brooke, Meeka, and Jolene wander off in one direction.

Me, Jenna, and Randi wander off in the other.

"Don't go too far!" Mom calls to us. "The bus will be here any minute. Then we'll go see the Little House."

I look across the lake again. Motor boats purr by. Buildings poke up through the trees along the opposite shore. It must look a lot different now than it did when Laura and Mary were here more than a hundred years ago.

I pick up a rock and think about what Laura wrote in that letter the museum lady read. How so many things change over the years, but the real things stay the same.

"Rocks don't change much," I say to myself. "Even after a hundred years. Even after a hundred *more* years."

I look around at the other girls.

"And I bet running down a hill with your friends felt just as good back then as it does today. And fighting with them felt just as bad."

"C'mon, Ida!" Jenna calls to me. "The bus is here."

"I'll be right there," I call back.

I hunt along the shore, looking for the oldest rock I can find. One that will stay the same forever.

The school bus rumbles into the parking lot, but I keep hunting.

"Hurry, Ida, or we'll lose our seat!" Jenna shouts.

"Coming!"

I snatch up a rock that looks older than all the rest.

Then I grab a few more and stuff them into my pockets as I run to the bus.

Seven rocks altogether.

# Chapter
# 9

"Hysterical marker?" Brooke reads as we drive past a sign along the road that leads to the Little House in the Big Woods. "I don't see anything funny about trees and fields and tractors."

"*Historical* marker," Jenna corrects her, leaning over the back of Brooke and Stacey's seat. "As in history? Ever heard of it?"

"Oh," Brooke says, slouching. "Historical. As in boring."

"Boredom must be popular," Tom replies, looking up from a pamphlet he got at the museum. "It says here hundreds of people visit the Little House in the Big Woods every year."

"Hundreds of *bored* people," Brooke mumbles.

"Look!" Stacey says, pointing out her window. "There it is! Laura's cabin!"

"Where?" Brooke says, gawking. "Ohmygosh! Look, Jenna. It's almost as tiny as your tree—"

"House," Jenna cuts in. She glares at Brooke, then turns to Stacey. "It's a little *house,* Stacey. Not a *cabin.*"

"Same difference," Tom says, tucking the pamphlet into his pocket.

"Oops," Brooke says, glancing away from Jenna. "That's what I meant. It's as dinky as Jenna's . . . *house.* Don't ask me how they're going to fit another kid in there."

Jenna's jaw goes tight. She looks past Brooke at Tom. "Tom," she says loudly, "do me a favor and tell Brooke that we'll have plenty of room for the baby now that *she's* not hanging around all the time."

Tom does a puzzled frown. "I'm sure she heard you loud and clear," he says to Jenna.

Jenna gives Tom a squint. "Thanks for being so helpful."

"I'm very helpful," Tom replies. "Just not useable."

"What's that supposed to mean?" Jenna asks.

"It means he's not your little messenger boy."

Brooke whips a look at Jenna. "If you have something to say to me, then say it yourself. Don't make your *boyfriend* do your dirty work."

Jenna's eyes go wide. "He's *not* my boyfriend."

Brooke laughs. "Your *crush* then. What*ev*er. You *do* still like him, don't you? Ever since third grade?"

Jenna sits back, her eyes bright and her cheeks burning.

I look at Tom. He turns away quickly. His ears are as red as Jenna's face.

The bus jerks to a stop near the little log house and everyone starts scrambling off. There are only a few trees around it, but they're tall and old and I wonder if maybe they're left over from the Big Woods. Maybe Laura and Mary even planted the seeds they grew from, just like Rachel and her sandbox seeds.

My mom and the other chaperones carry the picnic stuff to a shelter.

Mr. Crow leads the rest of us into the quiet little house. We're the only ones there.

The main room has a window, a fireplace, a table, and that's all. Still, we're squished because it's so small. Two tinier rooms are off to one side. Upstairs there's a loft where Mr. Crow says Laura's family would have stored their food for the winter.

"Imagine what it would be like to live in this small space with your whole family," Mr. Crow says.

"Nuts," Randi replies.

"Murder," Rusty chimes in.

"Look!" Joey shouts, pointing to the cobweb-covered window. An enormous spider is crawling across the four panes of glass. Brown and hairy. Like the ones you see on nature shows.

"Ta-*ranch*-u-la!" Joey says, wiggling his fingers.

"Common barn spider," Tom puts in. "Big, but harmless to humans."

A hand clamps around my wrist. Strawberry-scented breath blows in my face. "Somebody kill it!" Brooke cries.

"Anything for you, Brookey," Rusty says, picking up a stick that's lying near the fireplace. He tiptoes toward the window. "*Herrrre* . . . spidey!" he calls.

"Rusty." Mr. Crow frowns from across the tiny

room. "Drop the stick. Step away from the spider. *Now*."

"Spiders are good luck," Meeka says. "Remember? That's what Mrs. Eddy said when she showed us that quilt with a spider sewn on it. You'd be crazy to kill it."

Jenna huffs. "I've killed hundreds."

"Yeah, but that sucker's *huge*," Randi says, stepping closer to Rusty. "You'd be doomed."

"Rusty," Mr. Crow says again. "The stick. Drop it."

Rusty sighs. He gives the windowsill a sharp tap, then flicks the stick away.

The spider scurries onto the wall.

Close to me.

Closer to Brooke.

Four fingernails cut a crooked path across my wrist. Brooke screams and dives. She clings to Jenna's back like a crazy cat.

"Get *off*!" Jenna shouts, squirming.

Brooke hangs on. "Spiders lay eggs, you know!" she wails. "In your hair!"

The spider moves.

Brooke howls.

Jenna slips off a shoe.

She lunges toward the wall with Brooke on her back.

*Whack!*

The spider falls to the floor and scurries to a shadowy corner.

*"Jenna!"* Mr. Crow shouts. "I said to leave that spider alone!"

"I had to do something," Jenna says, slipping her shoe back on. "Brooke was freaking."

"Don't blame me," Brooke says, straightening her tiara and smoothing her hair. "I didn't force you to commit murder."

"Attempted murder," Tom says.

"It looks mad." Jolene steps closer to the spider. "See? Its hair is standing on end."

"Bad luck," Meeka says, shaking her head.

"For Jenna," Brooke puts in.

"Outside," Mr. Crow says. "Everyone. Game time." He holds open the door and shoos us into the sunshine.

"Been nice knowin' ya," Rusty says, giving Jenna's shoulder a pat.

Jenna jerks away. "I didn't kill it."

"You tried," Rusty says. "I saw the gleam in your eye."

"Yeah, work on your aim, Spidergirl," Quinn adds.

Rusty snorts. "Your aim, Spidergirl, your aim!" They gallop away, laughing.

"It's good you missed," Tom says, coming up behind us.

"Go away, Tom," Jenna grumbles. "I don't need one of your brainy lectures right now."

"No lecture," Tom says. "It's just that spiders are useful. They get rid of unwanted pests."

Jenna squints at him. "Right now you're the only pest I see."

Tom's face falls.

Jenna tugs me away.

"He was just trying to be nice," I say to her, glancing back at Tom. "Besides, I thought you liked him."

"I *do* like him," Jenna says. "But I don't want everyone to know it. And *I* was trying to be nice. But all *she* did was accuse me of attempted murder."

"Who? Brooke?"

"Who else?" Jenna says. "Some former best friend."

We catch up with the others in an open area near the picnic shelter. Mr. Crow teaches us some pioneer games. Drop the handkerchief. Shadow tag. Blind man's bluff. By the time the chaperones have lunch ready, my bonnet looks like it's been through a stampede. But I don't mind.

Jenna waves me to a picnic table after I get my buffalo burger. I sit next to her and what's left of her egg salad sandwich. Everyone fills in around us, eating and talking about the fun day we've had.

And actually, parts of it have been.

Quinn and Rusty are huddled across the table, whispering and giggling. I try to ignore them even though I wonder what they're talking about. I fiddle with the yarn around my neck and nibble at my burger. Maybe Quinn is telling Rusty what he said to me this morning. About looking like a tulip. About not stinking.

I hope he isn't, because there are some things you don't want to share around.

Quinn gives Rusty a jab. "Go on," he whispers. "Do it."

"Okay, okay," Rusty whispers back, glancing at Jenna. He holds his buffalo burger out to her. "Hey, Spidergirl," he says. "Dare you to take a bite!"

Jenna munches a carrot stick, studying the burger. She takes a sip from her juice pouch and squints at Rusty. "What will *you* do if *I* do?" she asks.

Everyone leans in, waiting for Rusty's answer.

Rusty takes time to think things through. Ketchup drips from his burger like fake blood. "If you take a bite," he finally says, "I'll wear your bonnet."

We gasp.

And giggle.

And shift back to Jenna.

"Will she do it?" someone whispers.

"No way," someone else whispers back. "She doesn't even eat regular meat. She'll never go for buffalo."

"Cluck, cluck, cluck!" Quinn does nose pecks at Jenna and flaps his arms like wings.

My eyes go wide. There's nothing Jenna hates more than being called a chicken.

Jenna's eyes narrow under her red brim.

Then she plucks the burger out of Rusty's hand.

And takes an enormous bite.

We gasp again.

"Whoa!" Randi says. "She did it!"

"Huh?" Rusty blinks. Ketchup clings to his empty hand.

Jenna smirks around the buffalo in her mouth. "Huh," she replies. Then she leans over her waxed paper and spits the whole thing out.

Triple gasp.

Jenna looks at Rusty and licks the corner of her mouth. "You lose," she says, untying her bonnet.

"But you didn't eat it!" Rusty cries.

"You didn't dare me to *eat* it," Jenna replies. "You dared me to take a bite. Which I did." She jabs her bonnet at Rusty. "Pay up."

"But that . . . but that . . . but that's not fair!" Rusty's eyes dart around, looking for the other guys to back him up.

"Actually, it is fair," Tom says. "She did exactly what you dared her to do."

"She did." Even Brooke agrees.

Everyone nods.

"Thank you, Tom," Jenna says. She gives him a smile.

Tom smiles back.

Rusty slumps.

Quinn snatches the bonnet from Jenna and plunks it on Rusty's head.

"Hey there, little lady," Zane says all twangy to Rusty. "You look mighty pur-dee!"

We all laugh like a tuba band.

Mr. Crow and the chaperones look up.

They see Rusty and start laughing too.

I catch Stacey's eye.

She lets a smile slip.

A real smile.

Brooke flings a skinny arm around Stacey's neck and reels her in before I have a chance to smile back.

Then she snags Meeka and Jolene.

The four of them flit away.

# Chapter
# 10

Later that night, I help with the supper dishes and take a bath and give my Lake Pepin rocks a shampoo. I line them up on the windowsill in my bedroom to dry. "Seven rocks," I say to George. He's watching from my bed. "Just like us girls."

Then I do some rearranging.

Three rocks here.

Four rocks there.

I look at George. "Do you think we'll ever be seven again?"

George stares at me with his black button eyes. Then he glances at one of the rocks.

I pick it up and set it between the others. "Me," I say. "I'm the rock in the middle. The one who has to get the other rocks to roll back in."

My stomach squirms a little. Like it did this

afternoon when we all got on the bus to head back to school after our class trip. Brooke beat me and Jenna to the best seat. Randi squished in next to her because she loves to win, even if it means having to sit with Brooke.

Without even thinking, I sat in Brooke's old spot, next to Stacey. That left Jenna with Randi's old spot, next to Rusty. But as soon as Rusty saw Jenna coming, he reached across the aisle and yanked Quinn in.

Jenna had two choices. Sit in Quinn's old spot, next to Tom. Or sit with the chaperones.

Jenna chose Tom.

Brooke made smoochie sounds at them all the way back to school.

I kept waiting for Jenna to shoot dagger eyes at her.

But she didn't.

She shot them at *me* instead.

The more she shot, the more I glanced at Stacey. I was still mad at her for ignoring me all week and for laughing at me this morning. But I wondered if she meant to give me that real smile in the picnic shelter, to make up for the fake smile she had given me earlier. And did she let Brooke and Randi beat her to the best seat? Was she hoping I'd sit with her?

I tried talking a little, to test if she wanted to talk back.

But all she said was "Mmm-hmm" and "Mmm-mmm." You can't have a conversation without vowels, so I stopped trying.

Jenna stormed off the bus when we got to school. She didn't say a word to me. She didn't even come home with us after school. She told my mom she had a stomachache from the buffalo burger she bit. So we dropped her off at home.

But I don't think a buffalo made her stomach hurt.

I think I did.

Because I ditched her to sit with Stacey.

At least that's how it must have looked to Jenna. And instead of trying to explain that I hadn't ditched her, I just pretended that I didn't know she was mad.

I rub my stomach. And look out my window. I can't see Jenna's house from here, but I know it's there, just a few blocks away.

And I know she's there too. Or at least I think she is.

Maybe looking out her window.

Maybe feeling squirmy about today too.

"You can't unditch someone," I say to George. "All you can do is say you're sorry and hope they yank you back in."

The telephone rings and a moment later I hear my mom all light and chatty downstairs.

I look at the clock on my desk.

7:46 p.m.

I'm allowed to call friends until 8:00.

My stomach does triple-flips as I hunt around for our cordless phone and take it back to my room. When Mom is done talking on the other phone, I sit on my bed and punch in Jenna's number.

*Ring . . . ring . . . ring . . .*

"Hello?"

It's Jenna.

"Hi," I say. "It's me. Ida."

"I know," Jenna says. "We have caller ID."

"Oh."

Silence.

"It only tells me your name, though," Jenna

says. "Not *why* you're calling. You have to provide that information yourself."

"Oh," I say again. "Um . . . I just wanted to tell you something."

"Uh-huh," Jenna says. "I figured that much out when the phone rang." She pauses and takes a breath. "Tell me what?"

"It's just that . . . I'm sorry about today. For ditching you. For sitting with Stacey. It was mean."

"You weren't being mean," Jenna says. "You were being honest. You'd rather sit with Stacey than with me. I get it."

"No, you don't," I reply. "I mean, yes, I do want to sit with Stacey. Sometimes. And with the other girls. *And* with you."

Jenna huffs. "You can't have everything."

"I don't want everything," I say. "I just want those three things."

Silence again.

"Are you still there?" I ask.

"Of course I'm still here," Jenna mumbles. "Where else would I be?" She does another breath. "I'm sorry too. For getting mad and for acting like the whole thing was some *ginormous* emergency. I'm surprised you didn't call 911."

I do a little snort.

Jenna does one too.

"Friends again?" I ask.

"Duh," Jenna replies. "I'd be friendless without you."

"You're crazy," I reply. "You have lots of friends. When we're not fighting."

"Now who's crazy? Do my *friends* save me a place in line? No. Do they meet me at the Purdee Good for cookies and ice cream? No. Do they call or send me e-mails? No and no again."

"I've called you a bunch of times," I say. "And I invited you to the Purdee Good just the other day."

"You've called me twelve times since Christmas," Jenna replies. "I can show you the dates in my journal. And the Purdee Good was a mercy invite. Those don't count."

I pause, knowing what I want to say next, but trying to pick the right words to say it. "Maybe if you weren't so . . . bossy . . . people would be more friendly."

Jenna does a sharp breath. "Maybe if people

were more *friendly,* I wouldn't be so bossy!"

I pull George toward me and wind his tail around my finger, thinking. I've always just assumed that everyone avoids Jenna because she's such a boss.

But what if I've got it twisted the wrong way around?

If everyone treated Jenna like a friend, would she be more of a friend too?

George winces. I unwind his tail. "Just because I want to have other friends, doesn't mean I'm not your friend," I say. "Besides, how many times have you called *me*? Or sent *me* an e-mail? Or saved *me* a place in line? I bet you don't keep track of that in your journal."

Jenna's quiet for a moment. "I don't have time to sit around and think about who's inviting who to do what when," she finally says. "All anybody has time for at my house is worrying about the *stupid* baby."

I frown. "Don't say that, Jenna. The baby isn't stupid. It's not trying to be a problem."

Jenna laughs. "If there was no baby we wouldn't *have* any problems. Don't you get that?"

She's quiet again. "Sometimes I wish . . . I *really, really* wish . . . that the baby would never be—"

I hear Jenna's mom calling her name in the background.

"That the baby would never be *what*?" I ask. "Born?"

Jenna sighs. "Just forget it. I have to go. But listen, there's something I want to tell you. Show you, actually. Something I promised to keep secret a long time ago. But I think the promise is worn out now."

"What is it?" I ask.

"You'll have to come to my house," she replies. "Not *at* my house. But close by. In my woods."

I think about the crooked path in Jenna's little woods. I bet that's where we'll end up.

"When?" I say. "This weekend?"

"No," Jenna replies. "I have to babysit Rachel and I don't want her to come along."

"Next week then," I say. "When Rachel has piano lessons."

"Good," Jenna says. "I'll put it on Tuesday's schedule."

I do a smile. I hear Jenna do one back.

Then I hear Mrs. Drews's voice in the background again.

"Have to go," Jenna says. "Little Precious probably wants a banana. See you at school?"

"Yep," I say. "See you then."

I set down the phone.

And wonder what Jenna's big secret will be.

# Chapter
## 11

The bell is ringing when I get to school on Monday morning. It's raining, so my mom drove me. I hurry to hang up my raincoat and backpack. Mrs. Eddy is setting a square of cloth with a threaded needle on my desk as I sit down. She sets one on Stacey's desk too. And Jenna's. And Dominic's.

"What's this?" Dominic asks, picking up his cloth.

"A buffalo burger," Jenna says, pressing her lips into a sassy smile.

"Very funny," Dominic replies. "I mean, what's it for?"

"Today you learn how to sew," Mrs. Eddy says, moving on to the next friendship circle and handing around more cloth and needles and thread.

"Sewing," Dominic says. "Yippee."

"That must be why they're here," Stacey says to Dominic, poking a thumb toward the doorway. Meeka's mom and Randi's dad are standing there, talking with Mr. Crow.

Dominic nods. "To teach us how to do it."

"Without drawing blood." Stacey giggles. So does Dominic.

I giggle too. But as soon as Stacey hears me, she turns off her giggle switch. Then she makes her face go smooth and blinks the sparkles out of her eyes.

I turn off my switch too.

"Now *that* would be fun!" Dominic fake pokes Jenna with his needle.

Jenna stops watching me and Stacey. She gives Dominic a shove.

"Settle down, everyone," Mr. Crow says, glancing at the clock above his desk. "Our helpers can't stay long, so we need to get started right away."

Heels click quickly down the hallway.

Brooke's mom rushes in. "I'm late! I know!" she announces, all breathless. "Traffic was *crazy*!" She sets a briefcase on Mr. Crow's chair and starts unbuttoning her raincoat. "And the weather? Ugh!" She pulls off her coat and gives it a shake. Raindrops pitter-patter across the papers on Mr. Crow's desk.

"No problem, Mrs. Morgan," Mr. Crow says. "We were just getting started." He picks up the papers on his desk and fans them in the air.

"There's crazy traffic in Purdee?" I say to Jenna.

Jenna lifts a shoulder. "More like crazy *drivers*." She pokes her chin toward Mrs. Morgan and twirls a finger by her ear.

Brooke looks over from her friendless circle and squints at Jenna. "Is *your* mother helping today?" she asks.

Jenna squints back. "You know she isn't."

"Oh, that's right," Brooke says sweetly. "She can't do anything anymore, can she?"

Jenna's eyes go icy. Her cheeks burn. "You should know," she says. "You can't do anything either. Except for say mean things about my family behind my back."

Brooke rolls her eyes. "That again? For your information, Jenna, I didn't say mean things. I said true things. And I didn't say them behind your back. I said them to your face."

136

"What did she say?" I ask Jenna when she turns away from Brooke.

"Yeah, tell us," Dominic chimes in. "I could use a laugh."

"Fighting with your friends isn't funny, Dominic," Stacey puts in. She glances at me and away again. "Especially your best friends."

"*Former* best friends," Jenna grumbles, shooting a look at Brooke.

"Fine," Dominic says. "Tell us what Brooke said, Jenna. I promise not to laugh even if it's funny."

"You're the last blabbermouth I would tell, *Dumb*inic," Jenna replies. "The whole school would know by the end of recess."

Dominic makes his face go all serious. He puts his hand on his chest like he's getting ready to say the Pledge of Allegiance. "What's said in the friendship circle, *stays* in the friendship circle." Then he leans in and nudges his glasses up a notch. "Go on," he says to Jenna. "Spill it."

Stacey leans in too.

So do I.

Jenna looks from Dominic to me to Stacey. Her eyes narrow. "I don't share classified information with the *enemy*."

"I'm not your enemy," Stacey says. "Brooke is. I'm just one of her troops."

"Yeah," I add. "If you and Brooke stopped fighting, we all would." I glance at Stacey. "At least, *I* would. Randi too, I bet."

Stacey fidgets and fiddles with her needle and thread. "Meeka and Jolene would too. They told me so this morning."

*Click-click-click.* Mrs. Morgan walks up to our friendship circle, smiling. She has the same smile as Brooke, only bigger.

She rests a hand on Jenna's shoulder, her fingers sparkling with rings. "Will you do me a favor, sweetie?" she says to Jenna. "Remind your mother that I'll be stopping by tonight to pick up the file for the school carnival. I want to get things *organized* for a change. Oh, and I'll need the paperwork for the auction too."

Mrs. Morgan squeezes Jenna's shoulder and smiles again. "Can you remember all that or should I write it down?"

Jenna squirms under Mrs. Morgan's hand. "I can remember," she says.

Mrs. Morgan laughs lightly. "Of course you can,

smart girl!" She clamps Jenna's shoulder tighter and looks at Mr. Crow. "Let's get this show on the road!" she sings. "Some of us have work to do."

Mr. Crow nods, fanning the last of the papers on his desk. He motions to the other parents. "Feel free to pull up a chair next to your student while Mrs. Eddy explains how we'll proceed."

Mrs. Morgan swaps smiles with Brooke. *Click-click-click* and she's at the reading corner. *Click-click-click* again and she's scooting a kid-sized chair between Brooke's and Rusty's desks. She sits down and tugs her neon pink skirt toward her knees. Then she checks her watch, drums her fingers on the back of Rusty's chair, and smiles at Mrs. Eddy. "Ready when you are, Francine!"

Rusty inches closer to Joey.

Brooke smiles at her mother and folds her hands. She holds her head perfectly straight like she doesn't want her halo to slip off.

"You'll find everything you need for today's sewing lesson on your desk," Mrs. Eddy tells us. "The needles are very sharp, so please—"

"Ouch!" Quinn sticks a finger in his mouth.

"—so please be careful not to poke yourself," Mrs. Eddy continues.

"Good point," Quinn replies.

"We'll begin with a basic running stitch." Mrs. Eddy demonstrates, pushing a needle up and down through a piece of cloth, leaving a little path of thread behind. "After you catch on, I'll show you how to do a blanket stitch. It's trickier, but I'm sure you can handle it."

We get busy sewing.

"Think of the stitches as little footprints," Mrs. Eddy says while we work. "Try to make each stitch the same size and distance apart."

I concentrate, making my needle walk up and down along a straight path without stepping off into the wilderness.

Mr. Crow and the parents wander around, offering suggestions and undoing knots. But so far, no one is having too much trouble.

Except for Jenna.

"Can I help you, sweetie?" Mrs. Morgan hovers over Jenna as she untangles her thread.

Jenna freezes. "I don't need your help," she mumbles.

"Excuse me?" Mrs. Morgan leans in.

Brooke glances over.

Jenna looks up and glues on a smile. "No thank you, Mrs. Morgan. I can do it by myself."

Mrs. Morgan's eyes sparkle, just like the diamonds on her rings. "So independent!" she says, tugging one of Jenna's braids. Her smile stiffens. "More like your mother all the time."

She clicks away.

Brooke leans across the aisle. "Pass me a scissors, will you, *sweetie*?" She flutters her hand at Jenna.

Jenna picks at her knot, ignoring Brooke.

"Maybe you should start over," I say to Jenna as Stacey practically skips across the aisle with a pair of scissors for Brooke.

"No way," Jenna grumbles, her face simmering. She glances over at Brooke. "Not unless *she* apologizes first."

"Good plan," Dominic says, looking up from his stitches. "Never be the first to back down from a fight."

I do a frown at Jenna. "I was talking about starting over with your sewing, not Brooke." Then

I look at Dominic. "What if the other kid is bigger and stronger than you? If you don't back down, you might get creamed."

Dominic shrugs. "If he's bigger and stronger, he's gonna cream you either way." He licks his thread and pokes it through the eye of his needle. "No guts, no glory. *No* apologies."

"But apologizing *takes* guts," I say. "More guts than fighting sometimes." I think about how skimpy *my* guts are. Do I have enough to apologize to Stacey for fighting, even though she chose Brooke over me?

Stacey leaves the scissors with Brooke and scoots back into her chair. "What did I miss?" she asks.

"Guts," Dominic replies.

"Ew," Stacey says.

"And how you need them," I add, "to tell a friend you're sorry."

"Oh," Stacey says. She bites her lip and glances away.

I set down my sewing and take a big breath. Then I look at Stacey. "I'm sorry about the other day," I say. "The pigpen incident. I didn't want to choose sides. I wish we were friends again. You and me. And everyone else."

Stacey studies her sewing for a minute. Then she looks up and nods. "Ditto for me," she says. "I'm sorry I've been so mean lately."

I do a smile. "Double ditto."

Stacey giggles. "Make mine a triple!"

I giggle back. "With marshmallows and chocolate sauce on top."

Dominic rubs his stomach. "Easy on the sugar, you two. I'm getting a *gut*-ache."

I roll my eyes at Dominic. And glance at Jenna.

She looks away, pretending to be very busy untangling another knot.

After Mrs. Eddy teaches us how to do a blanket stitch, she hands out more practice cloth and thread. "I want you to do three rows of running stitches and one row of blanket stitches at home each day this week," she announces. "Then you'll be ready to stitch around your handprints for the quilt and write a friendship word with fabric markers on each of them. After that, I'll attach your handprints to the tree."

"Stitchwork," Randi says, poking her needle

up and down. "Better than homework."

"Yeah," Quinn says, looking up from his row of perfect blanket stitches. "I could get used to this."

We take our stitchwork outside for recess. It's stopped raining, but the playground is still wet, so we have to stay on the blacktop. The boys call dibs on the basketball court. We girls have to huddle together in the only corner with no puddles.

Actually, there's one puddle. A small one. Brooke, Stacey, Meeka, and Jolene sit on one side of it. Jenna and Randi sit on the other side. They remind me of the rocks on my windowsill at home.

I know I should sit between them. The rock in the middle. But my butt would get wet. So I sit by Jenna and Randi instead. *"Please hurry and evaporate,"* I say secretly to the puddle. *"Then maybe everyone will scoot together."*

The puddle doesn't shrink.

I need another plan.

"I'm going to do *ten* rows a day," Stacey says, threading her needle.

"You don't get extra credit for doing extra rows," Jenna tells her.

Stacey shrugs. "I don't care. I just like sewing. It makes me wish I was living in pioneer times so I could go to one of those quilting bees Mrs. Eddy told us about. Where everyone sews, and chats about their cows, and drinks tea. That would be so sweet."

"Not unless you add a ton of sugar," Randi says, glancing up from her stitches. "Tea tastes like wet leaves. Trust me. I've tried both."

"We could do one at my house," I suddenly say. "A quilting bee. Tomorrow, if you want. I'm sure my mom won't care. Jenna is coming over anyway." I glance at Jenna. "Is it a plan?"

Jenna looks up from her tangled thread. "But we have other plans tomorrow, remember?"

I'm quiet for a moment, remembering that Jenna is going to show me the secret in her woods tomorrow. "I'll walk home with you *after* the quilting bee," I say to her. "You can show me . . . the thing . . . then."

Jenna thinks this over. "If we can ditch Rachel first, then . . . okay."

"Show Ida what?" Brooke asks, looking across the puddle at us.

"None of your *bees*wax," Jenna tells her.

Brooke huffs. "It better not be what I think it is," she says.

"It doesn't matter what you think," Jenna replies. "We're not friends anymore."

"Enough fighting," Stacey cuts in. "I'm calling a truce."

"You can't call a truce," Brooke snaps at Stacey. "*I'm* in charge of this fight. Not you."

Stacey narrows her eyes at Brooke. I don't see one speck of sparkle in them. She looks at Meeka and Jolene. "All in favor of calling a truce and doing a quilting bee at Ida's house, say 'Aye.'"

"Aye," Meeka and Jolene say together.

Stacey looks at Randi.

"Aye, aye, Captain." Randi salutes. "I'll *bee* there."

Stacey turns to Brooke. "Looks like a truce to me."

Brooke narrows her eyes at Stacey. "Fine," she says. "I'll allow *one* truce. But that's it."

"*And* one quilting bee," I say. "Tomorrow. At my house."

"Buzz, buzz," Randi says, nodding.

"We'll have to dress up," Jenna tells us.

"Yep," Randi puts in. "Yellow stripes and stingers. Wings optional." She snorts.

"In *quilting* bee costumes, not *honey*bee," Jenna replies. "Sundresses, aprons, bonnets . . ."

"Not tagboard bonnets, *pleeease*," Meeka says, glancing up from her stitches.

Randi nods. "Skip the bonnets. Plus, I haven't worn a dress since kindergarten."

"And aprons?" Jolene adds. "We barely have pot holders at my house."

Jenna slams her sewing on her lap. "Am I the only one with *any* imagination around here? Dig through your mom's closet. Tie a towel around your waist. I don't care. Just put together a costume and meet here after school tomorrow. We'll *walk* to Ida's house. Pioneers didn't ride the bus."

Jenna snatches up her stuff.

"Who made her queen of the hive?" Brooke grumbles as we watch Jenna march back into the school.

"Jenna would be queen of the world if we let her," Stacey puts in.

"I know she can be a little bossy—" I start to say.

"A *little* bossy?" Brooke interrupts.

"—but she has lots of good ideas," I continue. "And, besides, I think we should be extra nice to her right now. Because of her mom. And the baby. And everything."

"Um, I don't remember Jenna Drews being extra nice to *me* when *my* mom sprained her wrist skiing last winter," Brooke says. "I had to clean my and Jade's bathroom for a *month.*" She shudders. "Jade sheds like a cat. The shower drain was dis*gust*ing."

"This is different," I say. "Babies are bigger than shower drains."

"How would you know?" Brooke snips. "Have you ever cleaned one? Do you even *have* any hairy sisters?"

"No," I say. "But that doesn't mean I don't know the difference between what's a big deal and what's not." I look across the puddle. "Right now Jenna is the biggest deal we've got. If she's our friend, then we should treat her like one."

I grab my thread and scissors and stand up. "So we walk to my house tomorrow, like Jenna said?"

Everyone nods.

Brooke mumbles something I can't hear, but she nods too.

"I'll ask my mom if she's got any aprons we can borrow," Stacey says as the bell rings. "She wears them when she works at the Purdee Good."

"And I'll call my grandma," Jolene adds. "She might have some old dresses."

"My mom has tons of necklaces she never wears," Brooke says. "I'll raid her jewelry box."

I give Brooke a smile even though I don't think pioneer girls wore much jewelry.

But at least she's not fighting.

That's a big deal.

# Chapter

# 12

After school the next day, we all walk to my house. "Slow down!" Rachel yells when we turn the corner to my block. "I can't walk as fast as you guys!"

"Then run," Jenna says, glancing back at her sister. "If we don't hurry you'll be late for piano and Ida and I won't have time to . . . do something . . . after the quilting bee."

Rachel runs a few steps and then dribbles to a stop. "Why couldn't we just ride the bus," she grumbles.

"Because we're pioneers, Rachel," Jenna says, stopping. She reties her ruffled apron. "They didn't have buses back then."

"They had wagons," Rachel whines. "And horses."

Brooke takes off her floppy straw hat and fans

her face. "If we don't get to Ida's house soon I'm going to have a serious *melt*down." She wipes her forehead with the hem of her long flowery dress. "Pioneer clothes weren't meant to be worn over sweatshirts and jeans, Jenna."

Jolene's grandmother gave us a bunch of old dresses and hats and aprons to wear for our quilting bee. Jenna made us put everything on over our regular clothes before we left school.

"We could carry Rachel," Stacey says, straightening the fake diamond necklace she's wearing, compliments of Mrs. Morgan's jewelry box.

"Yeah, you could carry me," Rachel says, perking up. "Like a papoose. I heard about them in a book."

"A papoose was a baby, Rachel," Jenna says. "Not a kindergartner. And they didn't belong to the pioneers. They belonged to the American Indians. So start walking."

Randi shakes off her backpack. She sputters her lips and clomps her foot. *"Neighhhh!"* she says, crouching down and tossing her head like a horse. She glances at Rachel and sputters again.

Rachel smiles and hops on Randi's back. "Giddyup!" she cries.

Jenna frowns. "*I'm* her sister," she grumbles as we watch Randi gallop down the sidewalk in her T-shirt and checkered skirt. "*I* should be the one to carry her."

"You snooze, you lose," Brooke says, plopping her hat back on her head. She prances after Randi and Rachel. So do Stacey, Meeka, and Jolene.

I pick up Randi's backpack and look at Jenna. "Come on," I say, "or we'll only have time for a quilting *flea*."

I tilt her a smile.

"And no time to show you what's in my woods," Jenna replies, starting out again.

"Don't worry," I say. "We'll get there. Eventually."

We walk along and I point to the other girls. They've switched from galloping to frog hopping. "Look," I say. "Everyone is friends again."

"For now," Jenna says. "But Brooke will have them choosing sides in no time. Guaranteed."

"Not if no one plays along," I reply.

Jenna smirks. "If they don't stick with her she'll just find someone else who will."

My mom has a pitcher of lemonade and a plate of finger sandwiches waiting for us when we get to my house. The sandwiches aren't really made out of fingers. Peanut butter and jelly. Egg salad. Green olives and mild cheddar cheese. Small enough to pick up and pop into your mouth with hardly any crumbs falling on your lap.

We eat and then head upstairs. Jenna gets Stacey, Randi, Meeka, and Jolene organized in a circle on my bedroom floor. They talk and laugh and dig their sewing supplies out of their backpacks while Brooke takes a tour of my room. Fish tank. Bookshelf. Closet. Desk. It's all new to her because I've never invited her over before.

She picks up the noodle frame that's sitting on my desk. The one I made with Jenna and Rachel. "You should have used more wagon wheels," she says to me, jiggling one of the rotini until it breaks off. "They stick better. And glitter glue would have *looked* better. Not to mention sequins."

"Jenna told me to use wagon wheels too," I reply, walking over to Brooke.

Brooke sniffs. "Only because I taught her. Believe me, I was making noodle frames before Jenna Drews even knew how to hold a glue stick."

I think back to the last time I was in Brooke's room. A noodle frame was on her desk. Another one was on her dresser. A third on her bulletin board. Pictures of her and Jenna were in each one.

"Not much point in having a frame without a picture, though," Brooke continues, leaning the frame against my mermaid night-light. "You must have at least *one* friend who would give you a picture. Don't you?"

"Jenna promised me one," I say. "I just haven't gotten it yet."

Brooke huffs. "Typical," she says. "Jenna is an expert at making promises. Just don't count on her to keep them."

"She's never broken a promise to me," I say.

"Give her time," Brooke replies.

She studies all the stuff that's scattered across my desk. Pencils. Markers. Half-drawn pictures.

Books. Choco Chunk wrappers. "How can you live like this?" she asks, wrinkling her nose.

I shrug. "It's home."

"It's dis*gust*ing." She pokes at a misplaced baby tooth with my purple gel pen. I guess I forgot to put it under my pillow for the Tooth Fairy. "You need a professional organizer, Ida. *Me.*"

Brooke starts tossing wrappers into my nearly full wastebasket. She puts stray pencils back inside their jar. Then she blows dust off my lava lamp and slides markers into a drawer.

"You're supposed to be sewing," Jenna tells us. "Not cleaning."

"This is an emergency," Brooke replies, using a sticky note to scoop up the baby tooth. "If I don't do it, the National Guard will have to step in." She lets the tooth fall into the wastebasket.

The telephone rings downstairs.

"See?" Brooke says. "That's probably them calling now."

"If we don't get our sewing done it's going to throw off my whole afternoon schedule," Jenna replies.

"A *quarantine* will throw off your whole *week,*

Jenna," Brooke says back. "Is that what you want? To be stuck here? With all of us? Maybe forever?"

Everyone stops talking. They look at Jenna.

"Not if forever includes *you*," Jenna replies.

"Ditto, plus an eternity, for *me*," Brooke snips back.

She tosses a stubby pencil at my wastebasket. It bounces off and rolls across the floor.

Jenna picks it up.

"Don't strain yourself," Brooke says.

"Don't mention it," Jenna says back, tossing the pencil aside.

Randi sighs. "Here we go again. Just when everyone was starting to get along."

"I wasn't starting to get along," Brooke says. "I'm only here because everyone turned against me."

Jenna huffs. "Turned against *you*? They turned against me ages ago."

"We didn't turn against either of you," Stacey puts in. "We just don't want to *bow down* to you." She studies Brooke and Jenna for a moment. "You two aren't in charge of us. We're in charge of each other."

Meeka and Jolene nod.

So does Randi.

So do I.

Brooke crosses her arms.

Jenna turns away.

There's a knock on my door.

Mom looks in.

Right away I know something is wrong. Really wrong. Her eyes are too round and her mouth is too straight and her jaw is too square. Like she's wearing a mask of her face instead of the real one.

"Jenna," Mom says, stepping into the room. "That was your dad on the phone."

Rachel squeezes past Mom and flies to Jenna. She hugs her tight, mumbling against her shoulder. "Everything will be okay, won't it, Jen? Everything will be all right, just like you said."

Jenna holds Rachel awkwardly, like she's a bag of broken glass. She blinks at my mom. "What's wrong?"

Mom sits on my bed. "Your dad was calling from the hospital."

Jenna pushes Rachel away and stands up. "Where's my mom?" she demands.

"She's at the hospital too." Mom pulls Rachel onto her lap. "She's fine. Your mom is totally fine."

"What about my baby?" Rachel asks, looking up at Mom.

Mom gives Rachel a stiff smile. "He . . . was born . . . a little . . . early," she says slowly, like she's using tweezers to pick her words. "But the doctors are working very hard to make sure he'll be okay."

"He?" Jenna says. "It's a boy?"

Mom gives Jenna a real smile this time. She nods. "You have a little brother."

"Yippee!" Rachel bounces on Mom's lap. "I wished and wished for one!" She beams at Jenna. "Didn't you, Jen? Didn't you wish for that too?"

Jenna looks away.

I think about her wish. That the baby would never be born.

"He'll be okay," Jenna mumbles. "The baby. He'll be all right."

Mom reaches over and squeezes Jenna's arm. "Everyone is wishing for that now."

Rachel turns to Mom again. "What's my brother's name?"

"I forgot to ask," Mom replies. "But we'll find

out as soon as we get to the hospital. I'm taking you there now." She looks at the other girls. "Sorry, but you'll have to finish your quilting bee another day."

Rachel runs to put on her shoes.

Mom follows along.

Jenna unties her ruffled apron and lets it fall to the floor. Then she sits down on my bed. She pulls George onto her lap and twists his tail around her fingers.

I sit next to Jenna.

Everyone huddles in.

Brooke too.

Silently.

Sometimes even seven girls can't think of one thing to say.

Chapter

# 13

"Ida!" Rachel calls to me as she runs into the hospital waiting room. Not the hospital where Mrs. Drews is. We already left there and drove to another hospital with my dad and Mr. Drews. This one has a special nursery for babies who get born too soon. "I got to see the baby!"

"He's not *the baby* anymore, Rachel," Jenna says, pushing up the sleeves on the blue smock she's wearing over her clothes. Rachel is wearing one too. "His name is Tyler."

"Oops," Rachel says. "I forgot. Jenna got to pick his first name and I got to pick his second one. Any name I wanted as long as it wasn't Biscuit."

I give Rachel a smile. "Which one did you pick?"

"James," Rachel says. "Daddy told me that was

my grandpa's name. And when we called Mommy she said it would be a keeper. Plus, there's a nice boy named James in my class. Sometimes he lets me and Tess play connect-the-dots with his arm freckles. We make hearts and stars and flowers even!"

"Lovely," Jenna says, rolling her eyes.

"You should see him, Ida!" Rachel continues. "Tyler, I mean. He's tiny like a baby bird! Well, not *that* tiny, but still, he's very small for a person. And guess what? He doesn't have one bit of clothes on, but he's not cold because it's nice and warm inside his escalator."

*"Incubator,"* Jenna corrects her.

Rachel nods. "He's red and skinny and he's got wires and tubes and—"

"That's enough, Rachel," Jenna says. "You're making him sound like a robot. Besides, Ida can see Tyler for herself."

"Really?" I say. "I'm allowed to go in there?"

"No," Jenna replies. "Family members only in the *NICU*." She straightens her smock. *"Neonatal Intensive Care Unit,* in case you didn't know. But my dad took a picture on his cell phone."

Jenna walks over to where Mr. Drews and my parents are talking. She takes her dad's phone and clicks up a picture of the three of them—Jenna, Rachel, and Tyler in his incubator.

Rachel was right. He *is* tiny. And red. And skinny. Wires are taped to his chest. A tube goes into his nose. His eyes are covered with patches.

"Those are to protect him from the light," Jenna explains.

Rachel giggles. "Daddy says he's a baby pirate!"

Jenna frowns. "He's not a baby anything, Rachel. He's just a baby. *Our* baby."


It's dark and drizzly when we finally leave the hospital. Mr. Drews is staying behind. Jenna and Rachel are spending the night with us. Their grandma is coming tomorrow to stay with them until things calm down again.

We stop at the Purdee Good for something to eat. Lots of people we know are there. Even Brooke's family. Mom and Dad tell them about Tyler. Before long a little crowd is gathered around our table.

"Is there anything we can do to help?" Brooke's mom asks.

"Nothing at the moment," Mom replies. "They say it's going to be one day at a time until he reaches a healthy weight."

"It's lucky they managed to hold off the birth as long as they did," Stacey's mom says.

"Very lucky," Dad replies. "Any earlier and—" He glances at me, Jenna, Rachel, and Brooke. "Well, let's just say, that's one lucky little guy."

Brooke's dad rubs his chin and does a low whistle. "Think of the bills," he says.

All the grown-ups nod.

Brooke ducks her chin and glances at Jenna.

Jenna taps the table with her spoon.

The drizzle turns into rain as we head to Jenna and Rachel's house to get their pajamas and toothbrushes and Biscuit. Rachel is conked out when we get there. Me and Jenna grab an umbrella and take Biscuit to the backyard so he can run around while Mom packs up their stuff. Dad waits in the car with Rachel while she sleeps.

"Still want to take that walk?" I ask Jenna, glancing at her little woods. I do a half smile so she'll know I'm kidding.

"No way," she says. "Bears are impossible to see at night. They have very dark hair, you know.

Thick hair, too, so a little rain isn't going to keep them from prowling around."

"I was just joking," I say. "But, anyway, I don't think bears live in this neighborhood."

Jenna grips the umbrella tighter. "You don't know everything, Ida."

I look away. "Nope," I say quietly. "I don't. But I'd rather not know everything than be a know-it-all."

Jenna turns and squints at me under the umbrella. "What's that supposed to mean?"

I shrug. "Just that it's okay to know lots of stuff without always reminding people that you know it. Take Tom Sanders, for instance. Everyone knows he's the smartest kid in our class, but I've never heard him tell anyone. He just . . . shows it." I look away again. "Showing is friendlier than telling."

The umbrella tips a little and drops of rain splash against my cheek.

"I'm just as smart as Tom Sanders," Jenna mumbles.

"Mmm-hmm," I reply. "I know. Even without you telling me."

Mom calls my name from the doorway. Jenna scoops up Biscuit. We head to the car.

Mom and Dad get Rachel settled in our spare bedroom. I find an old towel and rub the rain off Biscuit while Jenna unrolls a sleeping bag next to my bed.

She teeters over it for a minute and then sits down hard, like she fell from a tree. Her shoulders shake and tears spill from her eyes.

"Jenna, what's wrong?" I ask, letting Biscuit go and tossing the towel aside. "Are you worried about Tyler?"

Jenna's chin trembles. She squeezes her eyes shut, but the tears still trickle out. "I'm the unluckiest girl in the world," she says, her voice all quivery. "I wished that Brooke and I would stop being enemies. We haven't. I wished my parents would stop fighting. They haven't. I wished we wouldn't have to worry so much about money. We still do. I even wished that . . . that . . . Tyler would never be *born!*"

A sound comes from Jenna's throat like a door creaking open. "But he *did* get born and now he'll know I wished it!" She sinks all the way down and sobs into her sleeping bag. "He'll *hate* me. Just like Rachel. Just like Brooke. Just like everyone."

Biscuit whimpers and sniffs Jenna's arm. She pushes him away.

"Tyler doesn't even know how to burp yet," I say. "He doesn't know how to hate you. Neither does Rachel. Remember how she ran right to you when we found out your parents were at the hospital?" I pet Biscuit and let him lick my hand. "People hardly ever hug you if they hate you. Plus, I don't hate you. I bet Brooke doesn't either. Nobody does."

Jenna cries louder. "J-just g-go away!" she stammers. "L-leave me alone!"

But I don't go.

I stay.

And keep talking.

"I didn't hear your parents fight one bit at the hospital. And I'm sure they'll figure out the money part. Grown-ups are in charge of that stuff."

Biscuit sniffs Jenna's arm again.

She's crying too hard to stop him.

"You're Tyler's big sister now," I continue.

"Rachel is too. Give him a chance. He'll be crazy about both of you."

Jenna buries her face deeper in the sleeping bag, sniffling and taking big jagged breaths.

I just sit there and rub Biscuit's belly and listen to Jenna cry until they both fall asleep.

# Chapter
## 14

Jenna and Rachel's grandma comes just after the rain stops the next morning. I watch from my bedroom window as they drive down the wet street. One stop at Jenna's house to drop off Biscuit and then they're heading to the hospital.

I think about Jenna and Rachel having to watch no-sound cartoons and draw in scribbled-up coloring books all day. Sometimes family stuff is no fun.

There's something else I'm thinking about too. The secret in Jenna's woods.

"It's probably nothing much," I say, glancing at George. "Just some old wind chimes hanging in a tree, right?"

George doesn't answer. He just stares out the window, toward Jenna's house.

I look out the window again and tilt my head so I can see the treetops in Jenna's woods. The sun is peeking through the clouds now, but I still can't see any secrets hidden underneath the trees.

"But if it's just wind chimes, why would she promise to keep them a secret? It has to be something bigger. Big enough to share with her best friend."

*Her best friend.*

"That's not Brooke anymore, George. That's me." I think for a moment. About how things have changed lately, with Jenna and Stacey and the other girls. And all the time I've been spending with Jenna. And how much time Stacey's been spending with Brooke. "Maybe Stacey isn't my only best friend anymore. Maybe Jenna is too."

I pick up George and study his smile. "I'm going to Jenna's woods. It won't be like I'm sneaking around, because she already invited me. Do you want to come along?"

George glances away. He's not a big fan of nature.

"Okay then," I say, setting him down. "I'll go by myself."

When I get to Jenna's house I ring the doorbell to make sure they've already left for the hospital. Biscuit comes running and barking. His claws scratch against the door with each jump, like he's trying to open it and let me in.

"It's just me, Biscuit!" I call, cupping my hands against the door. "Ida May! Jenna's friend? *Calm down.* I don't need to come inside. I already know the way."

Biscuit stops jumping and starts whining.

I scoot around back and head into the woods.

The crooked path looks more trampled than the last time I saw it. Like someone has walked down it recently. Maybe Jenna? But how could she? She's been at school or my house or the hospital since Thursday.

"Probably just squirrels," I say, darting my eyes back and forth between the sun-speckled trees.

"Or rabbits."

I gulp.

"Or very small bears."

I walk down the crooked path as quietly as I can, secretly wishing someone was with me. Even a stuffed monkey. Scary feelings are easier to take when you can share them with a friend.

I climb over a damp log.

And turn two corners.

Then I gasp.

"Oh wow," I whisper.

And gasp again.

There's a little clearing at the end of the crooked path. A big tree is in the center of it. It has four thick branches, like elephant legs, angling up out of the trunk. A tree house sits in the center of the branches, about halfway up to the sky.

It must be an old tree house, because the green paint on its walls is mostly chipped away. A branch is growing right through the mossy roof. Wind chimes clink in an open window. Another set hangs from a rung on the ladder that leads from the ground to a trapdoor in the floor. Bolts. Screws. Sticks. String. The same wind chimes Jenna made with me.

"A Little House in the Big Tree," I say. "Jenna's secret."

An acorn falls from the open trapdoor. *Shoots* from it, actually. Like some rude squirrel spit

171

it out. It ping-pongs down the ladder and then bounces to my feet.

I hear a swishing sound and look at the doorway again.

It's not the swish of a squirrel tail.

It's a bigger swish.

Much bigger.

*Do bears have tails? Can they climb ladders?* Suddenly, I can't remember.

*Swish! Swishhhh!*

More acorns fly. Leaves. Twigs. Sticks.

I stumble back, my eyes glued to the tree house and my tongue stuck to the roof of my mouth.

*Run!* My brain shouts to my feet. *Runrunrun!*

But the message only gets as far as the knot in my stomach. My eyes and my tongue and my feet stay put.

A shape flashes past the window. Tall, with long dark hair.

*Bear* hair.

I turn and make myself run. But not for long, because there are roots everywhere and one of them trips me. Trees can be like that sometimes.

I fall to the ground and taste wet leaves.

Randi was right.

They're not so good.

"You're trespassing," I hear someone say.

I glance up, half expecting to see a talking bear standing over me.

Brooke frowns down from a window in the tree house.

"I . . . I . . . I . . ." I stammer, sitting up and spitting leaves. "I . . . thought you were . . . a *bear*."

Brooke smirks, drumming her fingers against the handle of a broom. "Relax, Goldilocks," she says. "It's just me." She flicks her wrist toward the tree house. "Welcome to my humble home."

"This is yours?" I say, standing up and brushing twigs off my shirt.

"Technically? Mine and the FBF's. Former Best Friend? As in Jenna Drews. We found it last fall before she ditched me. Which, thankfully, she did, because I see she can't keep a promise."

"What promise?" I ask.

"To keep this place a secret." Brooke leans the broom against the windowsill and crosses her arms. "*Our* secret," she adds. "But here you are, so there you go. Jenna Drews is a big fat blabber."

"No she's not," I say. "Not a big fat one. She only told *me* that there was something in her woods."

Brooke snorts and spins her hands like pinwheels. "See? This is what I mean. Everyone says *I* talk behind people's backs, when it's *Jenna* who can't keep her mouth shut."

"Your back is the only one Jenna talked behind," I tell Brooke. "And she only did it because she thought your promise was worn out."

Brooke breaks a stick off the tree and throws it out the window.

I duck.

"Promises *never* wear out," she snaps, "even if friendships do."

I stand still and hope I won't have to dodge a broom.

"I'm just saying," Brooke continues, "people shouldn't automatically think you're one thing and nothing else."

"Uh-huh," I say, keeping an eye on the broom. "Makes sense."

Brooke smoothes back her hair and takes a deep breath, like she just swam up to the surface.

Then she gives me the once-over.

"Well, as long as you're here," she says, "you might as well come up."

The inside of the tree house is a lot like the outside, only no green paint. Just plain wooden boards for walls. Same for the floor and the ceiling. It's mostly empty except for a paper plate seed collage tacked to a wall and the broom Brooke was using. A pink plastic chair is shoved in one corner. Something is lying on the floor next to it.

"I love what you've done with the place," I say, turning in a circle.

Brooke squints. "Ha-ha. If I had my way, it would be totally *smooth*." She turns in a circle too, arms stretched out so her hands make a little frame she can look through. "Posters on the walls. Beads in the windows. Bright pink rugs on the floor. A beanbag chair or two."

"So how come it's not, you know, *smooth*?" I ask.

"Because of the big fat fight." Brooke plops down on the plastic chair.

I sit on the floor, crisscross applesauce, in front of her. "What fight?"

"The one that happened after Jenna and I found this place. We were taking Biscuit for a walk."

I blink. "In the woods? You? And Jenna?"

"Not *in* the woods," Brooke says. "Down her path to the park. Only, Biscuit got away from us. We chased him around in circles for*ev*er until his leash got caught on something *right* underneath the tree house. Weird, huh?"

I nod. "I've got goose bumps. Go on."

"We decided to make this place our secret hideout. So we ditched Biscuit at Jenna's house and planned a whole ceremony to make it official. We came back the next day to do it. I even brought friendship necklaces for each of us."

Brooke pulls a necklace chain from under her shirt collar. Half of a broken heart hangs from it. Two words are written on it:

*ENDS*

*EVER*

I frown. "Ends ever? That doesn't sound very friendly."

"Jenna's half said *FRI FOR*," Brooke explains. "When we fit the halves together it spelled *FRIENDS FOREVER*. Get it?"

I nod. "So how come you're still wearing your half if you and Jenna aren't friends anymore?"

"Duh, Ida," Brooke says. "It has a real *diamond* chip." She holds the half heart closer to me. A tiny dot sparkles on the tip.

"Point zero five karats," Brooke says, tapping the diamond. "It said so right on the wrapper. Jenna's half had one too."

"Wow," I say. "The only carrots I've ever owned are the crunchy kind."

Brooke sits back, twirling her chain. "Diamonds last forever, so we swore an oath over them to be *friends* forever. And to keep the tree house a *secret* forever too."

"So far so good," I say. "When do you fight?"

"I'm getting to that," Brooke says. She leans in. "After we said the oath, we sealed it with *blood*."

I gulp. "Whose blood?"

"Ours, silly," Brooke says. "Jenna brought along a needle and a photo of the two of us. We pricked our fingers and pressed the blood onto the picture. I practically fainted, but I did it. Jenna too. Then we hung the picture right over there."

Brooke points to the wall where the seed collage is hanging. An empty noodle frame is lying on the floor beneath it.

I pick up the noodle frame. "So where's the picture now?" I ask.

Brooke flicks back her hair. "We finished the ceremony and then started making plans for the tree house. Well, *I* started making plans. But Jenna just pooh-poohed every decorating idea I had. She said bead curtains and movie posters and neon rugs would damage the *natural integrity* of the place."

Brooke does invisible quote marks with her fingers when she says that last part. "What*e*ver. Jenna made a rule that we could only decorate with things we made ourselves, or that came from nature. Sticks. Seeds. Flowers. Ugh. I swear, she'd only allow a rug in here if we wove it out of grass and mud."

"But you like making stuff just as much as Jenna does. Remember?" I wiggle the noodle frame in front of Brooke. "You taught her how to make these."

"Noodles are different," Brooke replies. "They come from the store, not off the ground. Rhinestones . . . sequins . . . beads, fine. But sticks and seeds and mud? No thank you."

"So what did you do?"

"I, very logically, said that we should put it to a vote."

"A vote? But there were only two of you, so—"

"And since I was *older*," Brooke cuts in, "I should get two votes."

"And then?"

"And then Jenna basically had a fit. She said if I got two votes, then she got *three* because the woods belonged to her *family*."

Brooke fiddles with her necklace. "So I said, '*What* family? Your parents *hate* each other and Rachel hates *you*.'"

My eyes go wide. "You said that?"

Brooke does a quick nod. "I know it came out sounding mean, but sometimes the truth hurts." She glances away. "I hear my mom and her friends talking about Jenna's family all the time. They call Jenna's dad *driftwood* because he's always looking for work and her mom *Herr Drews*."

"*Hair* Drews?"

Brooke shrugs. "Probably because of her long

braids. But it's more the *way* they say it. Like the Drewses are a big fat joke, you know? So I told Jenna the whole town is laughing at her family."

"What did Jenna say?"

Brooke snorts. "She didn't say anything. She *shoved* me into the wall–*that* wall." Brooke points to the only wall that doesn't have a window on it. "I slammed against it so hard I practically broke my back. But that wasn't the worst of it. The wall was covered with spiderwebs. *Millions* of them. And every sticky strand was *gobbed* with ancient spider eggs. My shirt, my hands, my *hair*–my entire body was covered with them."

Brooke shudders. "Jenna knows how I feel about spiders. She shoved me into them on purpose. I saw it in her eyes."

"What did you do?"

"What do you think?" Brooke replies. "I shoved her back. We kept shoving each other back and forth until I *accidentally* grabbed her diamond chip necklace. The chain broke. The half heart flew."

I glance around the tree house. I don't see Jenna's half heart anywhere.

"Jenna accused me of breaking it on purpose. So I called a five-minute truce to prove I hadn't. We looked everywhere—inside, outside—but it had completely disappeared."

Brooke glances at the empty noodle frame in my hand. "That's when Jenna yanked our picture off the wall and tore it up. She threw all the pieces out the window. Then she told me that *I* was the joke of our whole school. That kids call me *tinsel brain* behind my back. Because of all my pageant crowns. I stormed out of here and ran all the way home. That's the *last* time I came to this place."

"But you're here today," I point out.

Brooke tucks her necklace back under her shirt. "Only because of what your parents said at the Purdee Good last night. About Jenna's baby brother and how nobody knows for sure if he's even going to . . . you know . . . live."

I nod.

Brooke sighs. "It just made things like diamond necklaces and pink rugs and getting your own way not seem so important anymore. Plus, when we got home from the Purdee Good my mom started calling everyone she knew. The school carnival committee. The PTA. She even called Mr. Crow and our principal. She told them what was going on with the Drewses and that something had to be done."

Brooke leans in. "But remember? My mom thinks Mrs. Drews is a joke. She always complains when they have to work together on a committee. So I finally just blurted out, 'What's the point of helping someone you hate?'"

Brooke sits back. Her chair creaks. "You should have seen the look on my mom's face after I said that."

"Bad?" I ask.

Brooke nods. "Scary bad. She grabbed my shoulders and said, 'I don't *hate* Mrs. Drews. We just disagree sometimes. Helping people is *what we do* in this life. No matter how we feel about them.'"

Brooke studies the floor. "So . . . I don't know . . . I felt . . . bad. For the mean things I'd said to Jenna. For fighting with her. For not telling her I was sorry a long time ago. I thought maybe if I came here . . ." Brooke's voice trails off as she looks around the tree house.

"Maybe you could think of a way to help her too?"

Brooke looks at me and nods. "So this morning, I dragged a broom up here to de-spider the place. And my old time-out chair because no way was I going to sit on this disgusting floor." She kicks at an acorn. "Then, just as I was getting ready to think things through, you showed up."

"Should I leave?" I ask.

Brooke blinks at me. She shakes her head. "No. Stay. Maybe we can think of something together."

I think about all the mean things Brooke has said and done to Jenna lately. Teasing her about Tom right in front of him. Telling her the school carnival will be a lot better now that Mrs. Drews isn't in charge. Splitting up our group instead of doing Jenna's playground good-byes.

What could Brooke do that would make up for all of that?

"Any ideas?" Brooke asks, fiddling with her necklace again.

"We could find Jenna's half heart and you could give it back," I offer. "That might help."

"I thought of that already," Brooke replies. "I

searched again this morning, but it's no use. Some squirrel probably carried it off." She looks out the window.

I nod. "A girl squirrel who likes sparkly things."

Brooke turns back to me, her eyes bright with an idea. "I could give Jenna one of my tiaras," she says. "My biggest, sparkly-est one!"

"Um . . ." I say. "I don't think Jenna is much into tiaras. She's more of a tagboard and glue kind of girl."

Brooke slumps and sighs. "There's nothing I can give her that will make up for my meanness. Even saying 'I'm sorry' might not make us friends again."

"It might not," I reply. "But if you say it, at least you won't be enemies anymore."

Brooke thinks this through.

And nods.

## Chapter

# 15

Mrs. Eddy is in our classroom when I get to school on Monday morning.

But Jenna isn't.

And I know why.

Mr. Drews called to say that Tyler was having trouble breathing, so the doctors hooked him to a machine called a ventilator. Everyone—Mr. and Mrs. Drews, Jenna, Rachel, their grandma—is sticking close to the hospital until he can breathe by himself again.

Mrs. Eddy passes around our handprint squares for the quilt and explains how we're going to stitch around the fingers for decoration. Later, we'll write friendship words on them with fabric markers.

Everyone starts sewing and talking about good

friendship words. *Silly. Smile. Honest. Pal.* But I'm mostly thinking about other words. The kind that are too big to fit on a fourth grader's handprint.

*Ventilator.*

*Incubator.*

*Neonatal.*

*Intensive care.*

I don't think Jenna should get stuck with such big words. Rachel either. Things are scary enough without all those letters.

"Keep working hard to finish your handprints," Mrs. Eddy says when it's time to clean up. "I'll be back on Wednesday to collect them. That will give me time to sew them onto the quilt before the auction next weekend."

My hand goes up.

"Yes, Ida?" Mrs. Eddy says.

"What about Jenna?" I ask. "She might not get back in time to finish hers."

Mr. Crow steps forward. "We'll make sure Jenna has a chance to finish. We're going to talk about her and the whole . . . situation . . . in a moment."

Everyone starts putting their sewing stuff into Mr. Crow's cupboard.

And talking about Jenna.

And her *situation*.

That's another big word to add to my list.

A hand squeezes my arm as I put my stuff away.

"Meet in the pigpen at recess," Brooke says. "Pass it on."

"What's the meeting about?" Stacey asks me when we sit back down at our friendship circle. "Jenna?"

"I think so," I say. "We haven't been able to think of a good way to help her."

"You and Brooke, right?"

I nod. "We sort of . . . ran into each other this weekend."

"At the tree house," Stacey says, nodding. "Brooke told me all about it."

"*Told* you?" I say. "I thought she wanted to keep everything a secret."

Stacey shrugs. "I guess she changed her mind." She glances around the classroom. "I might have mentioned it to Randi too. She might have told Meeka."

"If Meeka knows about the tree house, then Jolene knows," I say.

"What tree house?" Dominic asks, poking in. "The one in Jenna's woods? Yeah, we know."

"We?" I say.

Dominic nods. "Me, Rusty, Joey, Quinn . . . all us boys."

"Great," I mumble.

"Do you think Jenna will be mad?" Stacey asks.

"Probably," I reply.

Dominic shrugs. "Secrets slip. Life goes on."

"Jenna's family is going through a tough time right now," Mr. Crow says after Mrs. Eddy leaves. He explains about Tyler, even though everyone already knows. News travels fast in fourth grade.

"What can we do to show Jenna we care?" Mr. Crow continues. "Any ideas?"

Everyone is quiet.

Not one peep.

I guess most of us don't have a lot of experience thinking of ways to care for Jenna. Most of the time, everyone is too busy thinking of ways to avoid her. Me too, until I figured out there's more to Jenna than the stuff I don't like.

My hand goes up again. Two times in one day. That's a record for me.

Mr. Crow gives me a smile. "Yes, Ida? Do you have an idea?"

"Maybe flowers," I offer. "My dad says they can cheer you up when things go wrong."

Mr. Crow nods. "Flowers are a great idea. Anything else?" He looks around the room.

"How about a card," Brooke says. "We could make it out of . . . tagboard." She glances at me.

"Ooo . . ." Stacey says. "We could draw things on it that Jenna likes!"

"Like what?" Randi asks. "Sun bonnets? Egg salad sandwiches?" She grins.

"Yeah, we could draw a herd of buffalos eating them," Rusty says. "The bonnets, I mean."

Everyone laughs.

"She likes nature," Tom offers. "Birds, butterflies, trees—"

"Ta-*ranch*-u-las!" Joey cuts in, wiggling his fingers. "Those are natural."

"Natural *pests*," Brooke says, squinting at Joey. "Just like boys."

All the girls nod.

"Tell you what," Mr. Crow says. "If everyone works together to make the card—a big one with lots of trees and birds and maybe a *few* spiders and the occasional buffalo—I'll run to the greenhouse and get the flowers. One for each of you to plant in a container."

Brooke's hand shoots up. "And . . . who's going to pay for all of this?"

Mr. Crow smiles. "My treat."

"Make mine with extra dirt, please," Quinn says to Mr. Crow.

"And I'll take a side order of worms," Zane adds.

"Same here!" Randi yells.

"Me too!" Rusty chimes in.

"Got it," Mr. Crow says. "The works."

Meeka runs to the art room to get a sheet of tagboard.

She comes back with a whopper.

We fold it into a card and pass it from friendship circle to friendship circle, decorating it as it goes until it's covered with the craziest picture you've ever seen—an army of robotic dragonflies chasing a herd of tarantulas riding buffalos through a field of egg salad sandwiches. We write *WE MISS YOU, JENNA!* in big balloony letters inside the card.

Then we all sign our names.

Brooke's is the biggest, sparkly-est one of all.

"We're giving her flowers," Randi says later when we're halfway through our meeting in the pigpen. "And a card. Why do clean-up crew too?"

"Because I thought of it," Brooke replies. "And because it would be the nice thing to do."

"I'm not complaining," Randi says. "I'm just wondering why you suddenly want to help Jenna." She glances around our circle. "Some of us have noticed that you basically hate her now."

Brooke shifts her pretzel legs and pulls a clump of dandelions out of the ground. "Maybe I'm turning over a new *leaf*," she says, flicking the clump at Randi. "Plus, I don't *hate* Jenna. We just disagree sometimes."

I look around our circle. "So it's decided then? We pitch in and fix up the tree house for Jenna?"

Everyone nods.

"Only no pink rugs," I say, glancing at Brooke. "Or bead curtains. Or movie posters."

"Right," Randi says. "We go caveman on everything."

Jolene nods. "We could paint our own posters."

"And make seed collages," I say.

"A cardboard box for a table," Stacey offers.

"And logs for chairs," Meeka adds.

We all look at Brooke.

"Sound good?" I ask.

Brooke nods and beats her chest. "Ugh-ugh," she replies.

"When do we start?" Stacey asks. "After school?"

"No," Brooke says. "My family is going to the hospital. To visit the Drewses."

"Tomorrow then," I say.

Everyone agrees.

# Chapter

# 16

It's stormy on Tuesday, which is a good thing because it means we have to stay inside for recess. That gives us extra time to work on our handprints for the quilt. Mrs. Eddy is coming to get them tomorrow, but we still haven't finished sewing around them and thinking of friendship words to write across them.

Tom decides we shouldn't do any repeat words, and Brooke decides there can't be any capital *K*'s because she's no good at making them. Plus, every word has to get a nod from Mr. Crow.

It takes for*ev*er.

But we do it:

*Silly*

*Smile*

*Fun*

*Hug*

*Love*

*True*

*Pal*

*Honest*

*Goofy*

*Nice*

*Brave*

*Loyal*

*Helpful*

*Sweet*

*Unique*

Mr. Crow writes all the words on the board and then says, "Ladies first."

We girls start choosing the words we want even though we're not nearly old enough to be ladies.

Stacey picks *fun*. Randi picks *pal*. Meeka and Jolene take *silly* and *sweet*. Brooke looks over the list for a minute and then she chooses *helpful* even though it's the longest word up there. I see her glance at Jenna's empty desk after she chooses it.

Brooke usually takes the easy way out. But not this time.

I pick *loyal*. I think it's a good word for me because

it only has five letters. And *y's* are fun because you can curl their tails. Also, being loyal is important if you want to have friends because it means sticking with them, even when things go wrong.

We save a word for Jenna.

*Unique.*

Tom thought of it. I hope she likes it.

Then it's the boys' turn.

The Dylans go with *honest* and *true.*

Zane takes *goofy.*

Dominic, *nice.*

Quinn picks *smile.* Then he gives me one.

Rusty and Joey take *love* and *hug.* They wiggle their eyebrows at Brooke when they do.

The only word left on the list is *brave.*

The only boy left is Tom.

He takes it.

Everyone giggles a little because he's the smallest kid in our class.

But I think *brave* is a good word for Tom. He's bigger than he looks.


The rain stops when it's time to go home, but the sky is still rumbly, so we can't go to the tree house today. I ride the bus by myself. I sit by myself too. No Jenna to tell me the answer to number three on our math homework or to show me her afternoon activity chart or to let me pick the chocolate chips out of the trail mix she almost always has in her backpack. And the more I think about all that stuff, the more I realize that I really miss having Jenna with me.

I barely have time to get my school stuff unpacked and eat three cookies before the door-bell rings.

I run to answer it.

Jenna and Rachel are standing on my porch.

"Surprise!" Rachel says. "It's us!"

"Duh, Rachel," Jenna says. "Grandma called to tell them we were coming."

I give Rachel a smile. "I'm glad you're here," I say, opening the door wide, "even though I already knew."

When they get inside Jenna turns quickly to Rachel and starts unbuttoning her hoodie. "Piano," she says sharply. *"STAT."* She glances at me. "That means *right now*."

"Stop doing hospital talk," Rachel says, pushing Jenna away. "And stop undressing me. I'm not a baby." She undoes a button.

Jenna taps her toe impatiently and looks at her watch. "It's sixteen hundred hours, Rachel. *On the dot.* You should be sitting at the piano, ready to play."

"Duh, Jen," Rachel says. "Watches don't go to sixteen."

Jenna rolls her eyes. "Sixteen *hundred hours.* That's the same as four o'clock. If you paid any attention to Tyler's nurses you'd know these things."

"If *you* paid any attention to *me* you'd know I haven't learned my numbers past *one* hundred." Rachel undoes her last button.

"How's Tyler?" I ask, trying to change the subject. "Better?"

"Lots," Rachel says, shaking her hoodie to the floor. A silver chain swings across her chest. A sparkly *R* hangs from it. "Tiger doesn't even need an elevator anymore!"

"*Ventilator,*" Jenna says. "And his name is *Tyler,* not *Tiger.*"

"But that's what Daddy calls him," Rachel

replies, pulling her piano books out of her bag. "Every time we go into the nursery Daddy says, 'How's my little tiger doing?' See? *Tiger,* not *Tyler.*"

Jenna unzips her fleecy. "I should know what his name is, Rachel," she snips. "I thought of it."

"Uh-huh, and Daddy recycled it," Rachel says back. She hugs her books. Her necklace sparkles.

"Is that new?" I ask, looking closer.

Rachel beams and holds the *R* up to me. "Yep! It's got real imitation diamonds! Brooke said so."

"Brooke?"

Rachel nods. "She bought it for me at the hospital last night."

I look at Jenna.

She shifts her jaw. "It wasn't just Brooke. Her whole family came. Jade took us to the gift shop."

"Jenna could have had a *J,*" Rachel says, studying her *R.* "But she told Brooke *no.*"

I turn to Jenna. "Why?"

Jenna lifts her chin. "She just wanted to show off how much money she had."

I frown. "She was probably trying to be *nice,*"

I say. "Maybe she was even trying to be a *friend*."

"Brooke doesn't know the meaning of the word *friend*."

"Neither do you," Rachel replies.

Jenna's eyes dart to her sister. "Yes I do," she says.

"Nuh-uh." Rachel shakes her head. "Brooke kept trying to talk to you, but you wouldn't talk back. That's not being friendly."

"You don't know anything, Rachel," Jenna grumbles.

"Yes I do," Rachel replies, twirling her *R*. "Sometimes I even know more than you."

Mom calls to Rachel from the living room.

"Coming," Rachel calls back. She smoothes her *R* against her shirt. "When I get done with my lesson, you guys are going to help me water the sandbox. Okay?"

"It's been raining *all day,* Rachel," Jenna says. "More water isn't going to make those seeds grow. Nothing will. I've told you that a million times."

Rachel frowns.

"Actually," I chime in, "I saw a leaf poking through the sand the other day."

Rachel's face brightens. "Really?"

I nod. "You'd better check later for flowers."

Rachel smiles. "You and me are best friends, Ida. Okay?"

I smile back. "Okay."

"You shouldn't tease her like that," Jenna says as Rachel skip-hops to the living room. "She really believes those stupid seeds will grow."

"I'm not teasing her," I say. "I *did* see a leaf poking through the sand."

Jenna huffs. "Dead leaf on a deader flower."

I think about the pot of flowers in my bedroom. The ones my class is giving to Jenna. Me and Stacey took them to Jenna's house after school yesterday, but no one was home, so I offered to babysit them here. We couldn't carry the giant card too, so it's still at school.

"That reminds me," I say. "I have something for you. From school."

"Homework?" Jenna asks, picking up Rachel's hoodie and tossing it onto her bag. "Too late. My grandma already got it. Even my handprint for the quilt." She gives me a frown. "Who stuck me with *Unique*? Q is my worst letter."

"Tom thought of it," I say. "He said it described you perfectly."

Jenna's cheeks go red. "Oh," she says.

"And I don't have homework for you. I have a present."

Jenna squints. "A *present*?"

I nod. "From our whole class."

Jenna hangs her fleecy on our coat tree. "I can hardly wait to see it."

"There're fifteen all together," I say, showing her the bright red flowers in the big brown pot. "One from each of us. Plus Mr. Crow. He said you should probably transplant some of them because we really had to squish them together so they'd all fit."

I wait for Jenna to say something back. Something sassy like *I love how they droop* or *What a pleasant stink*.

But she doesn't say anything.

She just stares at all the red petals and green leaves and brown dirt like she's from another planet. Someplace where flowers don't grow.

*"Transplant,"* I say again, louder and slower.

"It means take some out of here"—I give the pot a pat—"and plant them somewhere else. In case you didn't know."

Jenna blinks fast like she's waking up from a deep dream. "I know what transplant means," she says, looking at me.

"There's something else too. A card. It's still at school."

Jenna gives me a suspicious squint.

"Really," I say. "You'll see." I look at the flowers again. "Do you like them?"

Jenna studies the flowers. "Yes," she says. "It's the first thing that was just for me and not for Rachel and Tyler."

I smile. "The pot weighs a ton, so I'll help you carry it home. Plus, I can help with the transplanting too. There's an extra pot and some dirt in our shed that my dad said we can have. I mean, if you want it."

Jenna just stands there, staring again like she's back in her deep dream.

"Unless there's somewhere else you want to plant them," I continue. "You know, somewhere in your yard . . . or . . . maybe *in your woods*?"

I say that last part in a sneaky way because I'm secretly thinking about the tree house. Maybe Jenna is thinking about planting her flowers there too.

"Yes," she says, blinking fast again. "I mean, no." She looks up suddenly. "I mean *yes,* I know where I want to plant them. Only *no,* not in my yard. Or in my woods. At least not yet."

I give her a puzzled look.

"Quick," she says, fumbling for her watch. "What time is it?"

I glance at the clock on my desk. "Fifteen minutes past sixteen hundred hours," I reply. "Why?"

"Four fifteen," Jenna says, biting her lip nervously. "That doesn't give us much time."

"For what?" I ask.

Jenna doesn't answer. She just bolts for my bedroom door and leans out into the hallway, listening.

So do I.

But all I hear is Rachel plunking on the piano downstairs. "Twinkle, Twinkle Little Star."

Jenna rushes back into my room and tries to pick up the flowerpot. "Help me!" she snaps.

Then she looks at me and makes her face go soft. "Please?"

"What are we doing?" I ask as we lug the flowerpot downstairs.

"Shhh!" Jenna whispers. "We're sneaking to the sandbox. *STAT!*"

"Flowers! Flowers everywhere!" The kitchen door slams open and Rachel bursts in from outside.

Me and Jenna look up from the pictures we're drawing and do surprised faces.

"Come and see!" Rachel shouts, pulling on Jenna's arm. A marker rolls off the table and I stoop to pick it up. But before I can toss it back into the bucket, Rachel grabs my arm too and drags both of us out the door and across my backyard to the sandbox.

"See, Jenna?" Rachel says, pointing to the five red flowers that poke up from the sand. "I *told* you the seeds would grow!"

Jenna's mouth does a twitch. "It was just luck," she says, glancing at me. "Right?"

I nod. "Luck and rain," I say. "Sometimes that's all it takes."

Jenna clears her throat and fiddles with her braid. "But they won't grow for long in all that sand, Rachel. We'll have to move them to a better place."

"Where?" Rachel asks.

"A garden," Jenna says. "A real one."

"We got a real garden?" Rachel asks.

"We will," Jenna says. "In a minute." She gives me another glance.

We run to the shed and bring back the extra flowerpot.

"Oh, look what we found," Jenna says, doing a surprised face again. "A flowerpot already filled with dirt."

"Magic!" Rachel says.

We help her plant the flowers in it. They look happy to finally be home.

"Five flowers," Rachel says, standing up and brushing dirt off her hands. "One for me, one for Mommy . . ." She points to each bloom in the pot. "One for Daddy, one for Jenna, and . . . one for *Tiger* too!"

She slants a grin at Jenna. "Right, Jen?"

"One for each of us," Jenna says. "Tiger too."

# Chapter
## 17

Jenna comes to school the next day and the first thing we do is give her the giant card.

We all crowd around while she looks it over.

Even the boys.

Jenna blinks at the pictures we drew on the front for a long time. Then she opens the card slowly, like she's afraid the whole thing might crumble in her hands.

"Did Mr. Crow make you do this?" she asks, reading everything we wrote inside.

I shake my head. "I thought of giving you the flowers. Brooke thought of the card. Stacey thought of drawing stuff you like. The boys thought of tarantulas and robotic dragonflies."

All the boys grin.

I see a smile skim across Jenna's face.

She glances at Brooke. "It's nice," she says. "Thanks for thinking of it."

Brooke does a quick nod. "I'm always coming up with good ideas. You know that."

Jenna does a little snort. "Like the time you had the idea to shake up a bottle of soda before we opened it? Root beer city."

Brooke snorts back. "That wasn't as bad as the time you had the idea to put regular dish soap in your dishwasher. Remember? *Suds* city."

They do a snort duet.

Stacey laughs. "You *both* know how to come up with good ideas. You're just the same."

"Yep," I say. "Only different."

Brooke reaches into her pocket and pulls something out. She holds a taped-up lump of pink tissue paper in the palm of her hand. "Here," she says to Jenna. "This is for you too."

"Careful," Randi says, stepping back. "Could be explosive."

Jenna does that suspicious look she's so good at. Then she takes the lump and unwraps the paper.

A silver chain slithers out.

A sparkly letter *J* dangles from it.

"It's not as good as a half heart," Brooke says. "And the diamonds aren't real. But fake diamonds are better than no diamonds at all."

Jenna looks up from the necklace. "But I told you before," she says to Brooke. "I don't want it."

"I know you don't want it," Brooke replies. "But I think you *need* it." She glances away and back again. "And I need to say . . . I'm sorry. For fighting. And for saying all those mean things about your family. And for teasing you about liking Tom . . ." She leans in closer to Jenna and whispers, ". . . even though I know it's true." She straightens up. "I wish we could be friends again."

We all look at Jenna. No one says a word even though our mouths are hanging open.

Jenna studies the necklace for a moment.

Then she looks at Brooke.

"I'm sorry too," she says. "For fighting back. And for always wanting to get my way."

She puts the necklace on and smiles. "Friends again?"

Brooke smiles back. "Duh," she replies.

Randi does a big sigh. "Finally."

Rusty nods. "Yeah, I thought you guys would fight forever."

"Same here," Quinn adds.

"Forever, plus two days for me," Joey puts in.

Brooke rolls her eyes.

Jenna lifts her chin. "That just proves how much boys *don't* know," she says.

All the girls nod.

"There's *one* thing we know," Tom says.

"What?" Jenna replies.

Tom twists up a grin. "We know you've got a secret tree house in your woods."

All the boys nod.

Jenna shoots a look at Brooke. "You told them?"

Brooke shakes her head. "I swear I didn't. I only told Stacey."

"And I only told Randi," Stacey chimes in.

"Don't look at me," Randi says. "I only told Meeka. And . . . possibly . . . Dominic."

Dominic grins.

"It doesn't matter who told who what," I say. "All that matters is that everyone is friends again. Right?"

Everyone nods.

By Thursday, we have the tree house mostly de-spidered. We decided to ask Jenna to help us fix it up instead of surprising her. I think that surprised her most of all.

By Friday, Mrs. Eddy has finished sewing all of our handprints to the branches on the tree quilt. She also used her sewing machine to make lots of loops and swirls on the background.

Only, some of the loops and swirls are actually *letters* that spell out our names in fancy cursive. At first, you don't even know they're there. But the more you look, the more you see your friends blowing around in the breeze.

And even though, technically, it's a friendship quilt, not a crazy quilt, Mrs. Eddy sewed a silvery web on one of the tree branches and stitched a spider to it.

For good luck.

And it worked too, because on Saturday we sold the quilt at our school auction.

Guess who bought it?

Mr. Crow.

Guess how much he paid?

*Two hundred dollars.*

Can you believe it? I never knew teachers were so rich.

Mr. Crow says he's going to hang the quilt in our classroom. He's even going to leave it up after we're too smart for fourth grade.

We got enough money from the auction and the carnival to finish paying for our new playground equipment. And enough money from the PTA bake sale that Brooke's mom organized to make Jenna's mom cry.

Not a sad cry.

A happy one.

I know because I saw her hug Brooke's mom when she gave her the money at the end of the day.

*Five hundred two dollars and sixty-seven cents.*

That last part was from me and Stacey. We put some of our spending money in the donation jar and split a giant cookie.

Sunday afternoon, we—me, Jenna, Stacey, Brooke, Randi, Meeka, and Jolene—meet at the tree house to finish the quilting bee we started at my house. The one that got interrupted because of Tyler being born.

The tree house really isn't big enough for all of us, so we have to squish together.

No one seems to mind.

We dig our sewing stuff out of our backpacks.

Also, cheese puffs.

And cherry whips.

Cans of soda.

And Choco Chunks.

"I've got big plans for this place," Brooke says, munching cheese puffs and looking around while we sew.

"Just remember," Randi says, "we agreed to go natural on the decorations." She beats her fist against her chest. "Cavemen don't wear tiaras."

Brooke wrinkles her nose and licks her orange fingers. "We're fourth-grade girls, not cavemen. Sparkles are a *natural* part of who we are."

"A few sparkles would be okay," Jenna says, reaching for a cherry whip. Her fake diamond *J* swings and sparkles on its silver chain.

"See?" Brooke says. "Jenna agrees with me."

"Actually, we won't be fourth-grade girls for very much longer," I point out.

Jolene nods. "Fifth grade, here we come."

"And then middle school," Meeka adds. "Do they even allow you to wear tiaras there?"

"I bet not," Jolene says. "I don't think they allow you to wear anything sparkly when you get that old."

"Agreed," Brooke says. "That's why we should make this place really *shine* while we have the chance."

"We could sew a quilt and hang it on the wall," Stacey says, looking up from the square of cloth she's stitching. "A friendship quilt, with our names sewn on it in sparkly thread!"

"I don't need to sew a bunch of names on a quilt to remember who my friends are," Brooke says. "Besides, Stacey, do you know how much work that would be? To make a *whole* quilt by ourselves? Ugh. I'd rather *marry* Joey Carpenter!"

We all laugh.

"I'd rather marry you too, Brookey!" someone shouts from outside.

We gasp.

And rush to the window.

And gasp again.

Joey Carpenter is smiling up at us.

So is Rusty.

And Tom.

And Dominic and Quinn.

"It's me!" Joey hollers to Brooke. "Your Romeo!" He falls to his knees and spreads his arms wide.

"And me!" Rusty adds. "Your *Rust*eo!" He falls to his knees too.

Brooke growls like a bear. "Go *away*!" she shouts. "Girls *only*!" She throws a Choco Chunk at them. But not very hard.

"Listen to Brooke," Jenna chimes in. "This is *our* tree house!" She lets an acorn fly.

Quinn yelps.

Sticks. Twigs. Cheese puffs. Choco Chunks. We throw it all out the window.

The boys duck and laugh and dive. Then they scramble to their feet and crash through the trees, scratching their armpits and screeching like monkeys.

Meeka peers through the branches. "Thank goodness. They're gone."

Jenna smirks. "I bet they'll come back."

I nod. "They always do."

When we get bored with sewing, we climb down the ladder and plant the rest of Jenna's flowers under the tree house.

Then I get out the rocks I collected at Lake Pepin.

We put them in a circle around the flowers.

Seven rocks all together.

I hope they last forever, plus two days.